Stilton Slaughter

Steve Higgs

Contents

Not Again!

From Peterborough, Albert could have caught a bus to the small Cambridgeshire village of Stilton, but he'd had one too many encounters with chewing gum on his seat to even consider it. He also had to consider Rex Harrison, his dog, and how he might be most comfortable travelling.

The Mercedes E Class taxi was plentifully roomy in the back for man and dog and the boot held his bags with ease. It was twenty times the price, when compared to taking the bus, but at seventy-eight, comfort was a factor Albert was willing to pay for.

He'd gotten lucky with the driver, a man who owned German Shepherd dogs and thought Rex Harrison was a cracker of a beast, even if he were a bit on the big side for the breed. Other cab drivers might have refused to take the fare, given the clean up all the dog hair might require, but not so Gohar, a thin man of Pakistani descent with a permanent smile and upbeat disposition.

The ride took a little less than twenty minutes with Gohar acting as local tour guide to point out a few features along the way. They were on their way to the Stilton dairy where Albert would be learning all about the famous cheese. It had been a favourite nibble of his for many decades, usually served on a dry cracker with a glass of port to sip. Imagining the flavour in the back of Gohar's cab, his mouth began to salivate, and as they came through the small village, he could see signs erected to celebrate the cheese.

There was to be a festival in two days' time; his arrival timed quite deliberately when a small amount of research revealed the event.

A smile of anticipation flittered across Albert's face; he'd never felt so free. Widowed for just more than a year, he missed his wife dearly, but the grief of her passing had faded with time and he no longer attempted to ask her questions in a forgetful moment. He was content to be who he was, and on this culinary trip he needed to please no one and obey no timetable other than the rising and setting of the sun.

His oversized German Shepherd dog, Rex Harrison, snored and grumbled, his head on Albert's right thigh as the dog stretched across seventy-five percent of the back seat. He was a trained police dog who held a singular record as the only dog ever to be forced from the Metropolitan Police for having a bad attitude. Looking down at him reminded Albert that he did have one other being to consider and that there were, in fact, items in his daily schedule: Rex's breakfast and dinner.

'Nearly there,' announced Gohar from the driver's seat, flicking his eyes up to look at the old man via his rear-view mirror. 'The dairy is just around the corner. Is that where you are staying?' he asked, feeling surprised because he didn't think it offered accommodation.

'No, Gohar. Rex and I have boarding just across the street at the Crown Inn,' Albert replied, looking through the front window to spy the dairy.

'Shall I drop you there instead?'

'No, thank you, Gohar. It really is just across the road. Rex and I wish to check out the dairy first.' In truth, Albert was getting hungry and the dairy had a small café on the side because they got so much tourist traffic passing through. Tours were a daily occurrence so a gift shop and a place to sample the wares were obvious additions for any keen business mind.

Gohar flicked his indicator on and swung his car through a ninety degree turn to bring it into Glebe Street.

'Oh, no,' muttered Albert. 'Not again.'

The Finnegan and Stout Royal Stilton Dairy bordered Glebe Street for a distance of at least one hundred yards as the various buildings spread out across the dairy's site. Pavement for pedestrian traffic ran the length of the street between the road and the property, and a low and ancient-looking red brick wall rose from the ground to frame the leading edge of the dairy. Two wide gates, a way in and a way out, Albert guessed, were the only breaks in the wall until it reached a row of terrace houses in the distance.

Opposite the farthest gate was the public house they were booked into for the next two nights, but the sight that drew Albert's eyes and caused his despondent comment were the police cars parked quite visibly outside of the dairy itself.

There could be no doubt they were visiting somewhere else and chose to park at the dairy; Albert could see uniformed officers moving about in the space between the wall and the buildings.

'Looks like there's been some trouble,' Gohar observed, eyeballing the police squad cars. He had to slow because they were nearing the gate to enter the dairy's visitor carpark. His indicator blinked, but he paused before turning in and twisted in his seat so he could look at the old man. 'What do you want to do?' he asked.

Albert wanted to find out what was going on, that was his immediate response. There were three police cars visible, which was enough to tell him something serious had occurred. However, it was the crime scene van and the distraught looking people he could see through the windows of the dairy office building that intrigued him the most. It had to be murder, only the shock of sudden and bloody death would get people so upset. That he couldn't see the coroner's van meant the body had already been taken away unless the van was simply out of sight somewhere deeper in the plant.

Gohar was waiting for an answer but Albert made him wait while he weighed up his options. He could go to the pub – his stay was already paid for – the dairy was most likely going to be shut for the day while the police dealt with whatever it was they had to deal with, but the festival would still go ahead and that meant even if he didn't get to see the cheese being made – his purpose for visiting the dairy itself - he could still have a great time. Thinking about the festival invited a new question though: what might be the impact on the festival if the dairy had to be shut by the police? Surely, the dairy would be working frantically this week as they got ready.

Albert needed to know, he decided, and he then spotted that the café and gift shop were still open, so he said, 'Drop me off here as originally planned, please, Gohar.'

'Very good, sir.' Gohar faced back to the front, waited for a car coming the other way to pass him, and then swung his cab across the road and into the dairy carpark.

'Here will do,' Albert announced when he saw Gohar open his mouth. He guessed correctly that the driver was going to ask where he wished to be dropped. Rex had been sound asleep for almost the entire journey from Peterborough, but he awoke now because Albert moved to get to the wallet under his right bum cheek.

Coming half-awake from a dream where he was lying victoriously on a bed of fallen squirrel mafia victims, Rex sniffed in a deep nose full of air. It was like taking an uppercut to the face and he shot up onto all four paws in surprise whereupon he bonked his head on the roof lining of the cab.

'Wowza!' Albert jerked in surprise as his dog went from asleep to alert in spectacular fashion.

Rex put his face down and tried to rub at his nose with one paw. However, there was nothing he could do to alleviate his symptoms. All he could smell was cheese and it was so powerful it filled his entire head. He identified it easily enough; his human ate it regularly at home and he'd sampled it many times when a bit dropped on the carpet or kitchen floor, or when his human put his plate down and foolishly left it unattended. This was on a whole new level though, and it felt like he'd jumped off a building and landed nose-first in cheese.

Keeping one eye on his dog, Albert handed over the required amount plus a sensible tip, and thanked Gohar for driving sedately and sensibly. It came in stark contrast to the recent driving he'd experienced in Bakewell, though he remembered Asim and his moving vehicle-law violation car with fond memories.

With his backpack over his shoulders and his small suitcase in hand, Albert led Rex toward the small café. It was on the end of the main dairy visitor centre which was a newish building that dominated the front of the dairy premises. Approaching the building, he got a few glances from the police – some of them were outside near their cars – but they weren't interested in an old man and a dog.

Just outside the café, next to a sign that said 'No dogs', Albert paused to adjust Rex's harness. Rex wore a jacket to show that he was an assistance dog in bold letters down each side. Albert had never qualified to get an assistance dog, so what Rex assisted him with was taking his dog everywhere he wanted to go. After years of service as a police officer, the loss of his wife, and because he was speeding fast toward his eightieth birthday, Albert knew he was being a bit naughty, but also knew it wasn't hurting anyone and largely didn't care for silly rules.

Now that his assistance dog jacket was sitting squarely down Rex's flanks, Albert straightened and went inside.

A little bell jingled above his head in that timeless small shop way he remembered from his youth. Back then, packaging didn't exist and going shopping meant the local parade of shops with butcher, greengrocer, baker, and newsagent. The modern, faceless culture where no one knew anyone could never be usurped for a return to the local friendly ways he remembered, and Albert accepted it with stoical silence.

Inside, the café had one couple in their sixties sitting at a table to his left. They had a tasty looking platter of cheeses between them and both were tucking in, their faces down to inspect the goods, and their butter knives in their right hands as if about to do battle with each other to get to the best bits.

Albert nodded a polite greeting as he went past and got one in return. Behind the counter, a brace of ladies in their late fifties were waiting to serve him. They were expecting him to take a seat at one of the available tables, but he kept walking toward them. Neither looked to be affected by the murder being investigated outside, which surprised him. In fact, now that he thought about it, he was surprised the café was even open. Had he been attending the scene of a murder or suspicious death when he was still a paid police officer, the first thing he would have done would be to empty the site of unnecessary people.

'Good morning,' he chimed as he came closer. The clock behind the ladies showed almost eleven thirty: a perfectly good time for an early lunch.

He got a, 'Good morning,' from both ladies though their attention was more focused on Rex.

Rex was sniffing gingerly and beginning to sort the scents into different categories. The whole place stunk of cheese, so much so that he was having difficulty separating out anything else. The only thing he did pick up, was a trace of blood on the air. Blood has such a base metallic note that he was able to pick it up even with the cheese blocking his brain.

'What we can get you?' asked the lady on the left as Albert looked at the two of them. Her name badge read 'Maureen' and to her left was Imogen. 'Would you like to take a seat and see the menu?' she asked brightly. 'Or do you already know what you want?'

Now Albert's curiosity really was piqued because they were not acting as if they knew anything about a murder. To his mind, in such a close-knit community as this small village – he knew it to have less than three thousand residents – news such as a murder would travel fast and everyone in the village would know the victim.

Nodding his head toward the windows in the direction of the police cars fifty feet away, he asked, 'Did something happen here this morning?' It was a direct question, challenging them to confirm or deny what had occurred.

'Oh, yes, we were wondering about that too,' said Imogen, crossing to the window to look out of it.

Maureen was less curious, staying where she was next to the till and the glass display of Stilton cheese scones. 'They arrived more than an hour ago,' she told him. 'I don't suppose it's anything interesting though. If it were, they would come and tell us. Now, can I get you started with a nice cup of tea?'

Albert found that he was now chomping at the bit to find out what might have occurred, but he was in the café and it would be overtly nosy to leave just so he could get an answer. 'Tea would be lovely, thank you. And I'll take two of these delicious looking scones with butter, please.'

Forcing himself to quell his natural desire to poke his nose in, he retired to a table where he relaxed and picked up a paper. It was today's, and a local rag whose front page was dominated by pictures of the impending festival.

'Is the festival a big event here?' he asked Maureen when she brought his food and drink to the table.

She placed them down, deftly positioning them so the handle of the teacup was poking out where his right hand would naturally reach for it, and then carefully placed his butter knife alongside his plate before standing back a pace. Only then did she answer. 'Goodness, yes. It's the biggest day of the year in these parts. Bigger than Christmas. People flock in from all over, and the village, because it's small, becomes standing room only. All the inns and hotels for miles around get booked up and the pubs and restaurants make a killing. This place will be overrun by late tomorrow, and we'll only just be setting up then. The festival doesn't start until midday on Saturday when they hold the great cheese rolling race.' She sounded incredibly proud to be part of the history of her village.

He'd heard of the cheese rolling. He'd even seen it on television at some point in the past. Whole Stiltons would be raced through the village for a distance of half a mile, each team competing against the others for a tiny trophy and bragging rights. Albert was keen to see it for himself and knew it was just a way to draw in more people.

He split his scone with both thumbs, knowing that to cut one's scone with a knife was just poor form as well as bad etiquette, then buttered it liberally and tucked in. It was sublime. Maureen heated it, as was the tradition, so his butter melted into the soft, crumb texture of the Stilton cheese flavoured snack. Two scones were more than he needed but he devoured them both with ease before sliding the plate over the side of the table for Rex to get the crumbs and butter drips.

Of course, he'd picked the table and his seat at it quite deliberately because it gave him a view over the forecourt of the dairy. He watched the activity outside like a hawk, his long-distance vision as good as it had ever been even if he was blind as a bat up close.

There wasn't a lot to see though. The squad cars just sat there. Every now and then, he would see one of the officers come outside to either get something from a car or put something into it, but he didn't manage to learn anything in the thirty minutes he spent watching.

There was nothing else for it; he was going to have to try the direct approach. With nothing to lose, he pushed back his chair, thanked the ladies for the food while commenting on how nice it was, bade them a good day and went back outside.

His dairy tour was booked for the following morning but popping into the visitors' centre to confirm it and then perhaps ask a few more questions didn't seem unreasonable, so that was what he did. Or would have done if Rex had let him.

Call of Nature

R ex needed to find a handy patch of grass and had been waiting patiently since they left the train. His needs were not going to wait much longer though, so he tugged meaningfully at his human's arm the moment they got outside.

He could see trees across the street and that almost always meant grass. Either they went there, or he went right here, and neither of them wanted that.

'What is it, boy?' asked Albert when he tried to go left, and his right arm went right. 'I need to go this way to the visitor's centre.'

Rex gave his human a meaningful look; he was usually more intuitive than this. 'Well, I have a pressing need to go across the road and when I say I have a pressing need, I'm not joking.'

'Call of nature?' Albert guessed. 'I guess the visitors' centre can wait.'

Rex walked as quickly as he could and even ignored the flash of squirrel tail he saw as it vanished up a tree. Off the lead, he ran, found his spot, and wandered back a few short minutes later once he'd patrolled the new territory and marked all the trees. It was his now, and no squirrel should dare to venture into it.

Albert fished out a baggie and dealt with the less than pleasant task of cleaning up after his dog, then clipped Rex's lead back onto his collar. 'Are you ready now, boy?'

Rex narrowed his eyes. 'You get to go whenever you want but feel that I should go when it is convenient to you. How about if I start going when I want, huh? Shall we try that and see how swiftly your attitude changes?' Not bothering to wait for a response, mostly because he knew his human was too dumb to understand what he was attempting to impart, he tugged his arm again and started back toward the dairy. 'There's a smell of blood over here. I think we should check it out.'

Sniffing out clues and finding the bad person had always been Rex's favourite part of police work. He'd been good at it too. Too good perhaps because he always solved the crime before the humans could work it out and would then get in trouble for biting the guilty person while everyone else was still trying to piece together the clues.

At the visitors' centre, Albert put his hand out to open the doors, but they swished open before he could get to them, the automatic sensor clearing the way to welcome him inside. It was devoid of visitors inside and only one member of staff was visible: a young woman, probably a teenager, looking bored next to a cash register at the far end of the space. Along the walls were Stilton cheese related gifts: fridge magnets, postcards, and books, plus all manner of other paraphernalia. He walked past it all being led by Rex, but his feet slowed when he saw the large computer screen behind the young woman's head.

'All Dairy Tours Cancelled' scrolled onto the screen from the right to pause in the middle where it flashed three times before continuing on its way to scroll off the left-hand edge and vanish. Then it reappeared again from the right on a perpetual loop.

'Why are the tours cancelled?' he asked the young woman once he got his feet moving again.

The bored-looking woman shrugged her shoulders. She was slouched on a stool with her feet on a bar so her knees were drawn up to form a flat surface. On her knees she had a small tablet on which she appeared to be watching television. She paused it with a tap of one immaculately manicured fake talon and popped out one of her earbuds so she could hear the old man properly.

'Dunno,' she said. 'Mrs Graves was upset about something, but she didn't say what it was. All the managers have gone into an emergency meeting of some kind.'

'But there're no tours today?' he sought to confirm.

The young woman swivelled in her seat and made a big show of looking at the message flashing on the screen behind her. 'That's what it says,' she said with an obnoxious smile. He'd interrupted *Love Island* and Sammy was just about to sneak into the waterfall lagoon with Richard. Those two had been flirting mercilessly since the first episode and she secretly believed they were meeting off camera for nookie when the viewers weren't looking. If the old man would just go away, she could get back to watching it.

'Will there be any tours tomorrow?' he asked. He had a feeling this was all going to be bad news, which felt desperately unfair given the distance he'd travelled to get here.

Trying (barely) to hide her annoyance, she turned to look at the screen behind her. 'All tours are cancelled,' she repeated. 'Now you know as much as I do.'

Albert bit back his retort. The young woman was rude, and it made him feel like being rude too. He took a breath and forced himself to rise above it. Leaning forward enough that the young woman had to lean back, he said, 'Thank you for being so helpful. I expect the customer service award will be yours any day now.' Then he left her before she could reply, but he needn't have bothered; she went back to *Love Island* the moment his back was turned.

Outside, he looked about for another member of staff. The young lady's disinterest actually gave him an excuse to poke about some more. He didn't get a straight answer from her but had already paid for his tour tomorrow and was going to act the role of disappointed, perhaps even disgruntled, customer.

All he could see were cops though.

Rex had his nose up. The cheese stench was still overwhelming, but he was starting to get used to it and could make out different smells in between. He could smell milk for a start. Lots and lots of it, and he was getting a whiff of deodorant from the human in uniform standing near a police car just upwind. The blood was proving elusive, like there wasn't as much of it as he previously thought, or the source of it had been removed, leaving nothing but the faint traces he now smelled.

Giving up on trying to find a member of dairy staff, Albert put his backpack and suitcase down outside the visitors' centre and approached the only person he could see.

The young male cop saw him coming and frowned. 'Are those your bags, sir?'

'Yes, thank you. Are you about to berate me for abandoning them?'

'It is best practice to keep one's belongings at one's side at all times, sir. They could be considered suspicious.' He was being lecturey for no good reason, so far as Albert was concerned and he was bored carrying them.

The cop made the mistake of not giving an instruction or asking a question; a sin Albert would have reprimanded him for if he were still serving, but the young man's inexperience gave him an opening to ignore the bags and ask a question. 'What happened here? It just says all the tours are off and the young lady in the visitors centre isn't being helpful.'

'It's a police matter, I'm afraid, sir. You'll have to move along.' The officer said it in a tone that suggested he expected immediate compliance.

'What's a police matter?' Albert shot back instantly. 'Was there a murder?'

The cop's eyes widened in shock, which Albert had been watching for. It made him think maybe it wasn't a murder. The young man looked barely old enough to be wearing the uniform. His face was shaved clean, but he didn't look to have enough facial hair to justify shaving more than once a month. He was taller than Albert, but a lot of men are, though he was only a shade over six feet by Albert's expert 'cop' eye and he looked nervous, or possibly unsure of himself. Of West Indian descent, the young man was handsome and lean – easy traits to maintain when young – and to Albert's mind, he looked like a cricket player whose name currently escaped him.

Next to him, Rex chose to sit, his nose up still as he sniffed the air. 'It's not a murder. There's not enough blood,' he observed, his small chuffing noises ignored by the two men above him. 'Might be a nasty injury though.'

Albert didn't think he was going to get much out of the man but before he got the chance to press him any further, people – cops and what Albert took to be the Dairy management – came out through a set of double doors.

They were standing in front of the old part of the dairy, the bit where all the work happened and where the offices dominated the front of

17

the building. Like any serious business, it needed to have someone managing the accounts, it needed a person in charge, and then people working under that person to deliver the various elements of the big plan.

As the people spilled out, some of them were arguing.

All the Cheese

'Chief Inspector it is not just for my sake or the dairy's sake that I ask for swift work. The entire village revolves around this festival. We have to get the cheese back in the next twenty-four hours.' The person speaking was a man in his late sixties wearing a tweed suit. His hair was a tidy, short-cropped mop of silver with a few dashes of black. If Albert had to guess, he would identify him as the man in charge of the whole operation.

The chief inspector, easily identifiable because of his uniform, looked aggravated. 'Mr Brenner, I already assured you we would do all we can to expedite the solution to this crime, but the theft of some cheese is not my principle concern when I have murders, rapes, arson, child abuse and other issues to deal with in Peterborough.'

His words, while pertinent and undoubtedly true, were not received well. 'Some cheese? Some cheese!' Mr Brenner raged, spittle flying from his lips. 'It's all the cheese! Over two thousand whole Stiltons at various stages of maturity have all been stolen, man. They are the worldwide king of cheeses. Calling them some cheese is like calling the crown jewels just some pretty trinkets. I'd bet you'd get off your backside if the crown jewels went missing!'

The chief inspector was not about to be spoken down to in this manner. Not ever, and certainly not in front of his subordinates. Rounding on the elder man, he took a step into his personal space. 'This case will be pursued with the diligence every case deserves. A man was injured in a violent robbery and a high value of goods was taken. The nature of the goods is insignificant. You ask me to guarantee you the return of your stolen goods within twenty-four hours when I have nothing to go on other than the testimony of one security guard with a head injury. He may prove pivotal, but the recovery rate for stolen goods, especially perishable ones, is measured as a single figure percentage.' He glared at Mr Brenner, who, uncowed just glared back. 'And don't you ever question my motivation or effort again.'

The chief inspector about faced and got into a squad car. Moments later only one police car remained; that of the young officer Albert had briefly spoken with.

The air between the members of the dairy management was tense, and no one was speaking. Albert doubted they intended for him, or anyone, to overhear that all the Stilton had been stolen in a raid, but he had. At least now he knew why the tours were off – there was nothing to see.

'Hello,' he said brightly. 'I have a tour booked for tomorrow. Shall I assume that it is not going to happen?'

Mr Brenner swung his head to look at the old man, then turned away and walked inside without speaking. It was a woman who picked up the task of responding, coming over to do so in person as her colleagues - half a dozen of them – all went back inside.

'I'm sorry, sir. I guess you overheard that we were raided last night. It'll be all over the news by tonight, I'm sure. I'm afraid there won't be any tours for a few weeks while we try to restock our shelves.'

'I see,' Albert said, because he felt he needed to say something. His mind was whirring away as he considered the problem. Who would steal all the Stilton? It was a good question that must have a limited number of answers. 'Did I hear that two thousand whole Stiltons were stolen?'

'They are just doing an inventory now, but I think it was more than that. They took all of them. We make fresh every day just to keep up with demand and ship them all over the world. The aging process to get them to maturity takes three months so we always have a large stock here. The insurance will cover it, of course, but it's the Festival on Saturday and we have no cheese for it. We made twice as much back in the summer, putting on double shifts so they would be mature on time. I don't know what we'll do now. I must go, actually. There is an emergency meeting to see what we can do to save ourselves and the festival. If you go to the visitors' centre, Matilda will be able to help you.

'Matilda?' he echoed. 'Young woman with a face like a smacked bum?'

The woman skewed her face as if to say that she agreed with his description but wasn't going to do so vocally. 'She should be able to help you,' the woman repeated.

'Yes. Actually, she wasn't very helpful at all. She spoke about someone called Mrs Graves.'

The woman made an angry face. 'I'm Mrs Graves. Matilda is my daughter and she's the laziest little so and so I ever met.' Mrs Graves looked like she wanted to visit the visitors' centre to give her daughter a jolly good speaking to. 'I'm really sorry. I truly must go. Was your visit for today?'

'No. It's tomorrow.'

'Please come back in the morning if you are able. I doubt we'll be able to restart the tours, but I'll give you a refund then if that's acceptable.'

Albert nodded his head as a salute of thanks. It was a generous offer to be making in a tough situation. 'That's very gracious of you. Please, you should go.'

Mrs Graves dipped her head in thanks and bustled inside at speed.

It left Albert outside with the young officer. 'How badly injured was the man?'

'Not bad,' the officer replied automatically. 'He got a whack on the head which bled a lot. But he seemed alright when I spoke to him.'

Albert sucked on his lips for a moment in thought. The cop seemed like a decent enough chap, but he'd just revealed pertinent information to a complete stranger without the slightest effort on Albert's part.

'Young man, I thank you for giving me that detail, but you really shouldn't be talking about an open case like that.' The man's eyes flared in fear and his cheeks burned bright red as he realised what he'd done. Albert waved a hand to calm him down. 'Don't worry. I used to be a cop a long time ago. It's a learning process. Are you the local bobby?'

'No. I mean, yes,' the man stammered. 'What I mean is, I am until Monday. The guy who is the local cop just retired. I was assigned here a year ago when I finished training and I think the intention is that this will be my beat one day. I grew up here and I guess I'm okay with staying in the village, but until the new sergeant arrives on Monday - he's being reassigned from Newcastle - I am the only officer in the village.'

'Albert Smith,' Albert took a step forward and put out his hand. 'Retired Detective Superintendent.'

The man took it. 'Police Constable Oxford Shaw.'

'Oxford?' Albert echoed, confused. 'Is that your first name? Or do you have a double-barrelled last name; Oxford-Shaw?'

'It's my first name,' Oxford admitted with a smile. 'My parents met there when they were both at Oxford university and they both watched Inspector Morse on the TV. I think it was a big thing when I was born and so I got the name. At least I'm not called Dave because there are dozens of them around here.

Albert decided to see how sharp Oxford was. 'Is that the name of the injured man too?'

'Yes, Dave Thornwell.' Again, Oxford replied automatically as if this were a conversation with his mates down the pub. Albert gave him a moment to see what he had done, waiting and not speaking with a questioning face to clue the boy along. 'Oh, God, I did it again, didn't I?'

'It's something to watch for. You'll get the hang of it. Where did they take him?' Albert fired in another question.

Oxford wagged a finger. 'Ha! You're not getting me three times in a row, Albert.'

Albert pulled a horrified face. 'But now I need to know where I can find him, Oxford. I plan to send the poor man some flowers.'

Oxford looked embarrassed at his mistake. 'Sorry. Sorry, he was taken to accident and emergency in Peterborough. That's the nearest worthwhile hospital.

Albert face palmed. 'You really are terrible at this, Oxford. Your answer should have been to tell me pertinent parties have been informed but details and news regarding the victim are being limited to immediate next of kin at this time.' The poor cop looked out of his depth and Albert felt sorry for him. It gave him an idea. 'Young man, what are you expected to do next?'

Oxford had to think about that. 'I don't know. Maybe hang around here? The chief inspector didn't say.'

'Then you should use your initiative. Let's use your local contacts and ask a few questions. You might turn up something that will help with the investigation.'

It was clear that the idea of doing some police work hadn't occurred to PC Shaw at any stage, yet Albert was here and had nothing better to do with his time. There was a crime and a potential disaster unfolding if the cheese could not be tracked down in time for the festival. Albert's only reason for coming here was the cheese, so since it wasn't where it was supposed to be, he might as well work out where it had gone.

Witness Interview

A lbert had all kinds of ideas about who he wanted to talk to and where he wanted to go. The Stilton had to be kept at a steady temperature or it would ruin, so the thieves had to own, or have stolen, rented, or otherwise obtained, a temperature-controlled van.

'How much space will two thousand Stiltons require?' Albert asked. 'How much will they weigh for that matter?'

Oxford was driving his squad car as they wove along the Cambridgeshire country lanes on their way to Peterborough. At the question, he glanced across. 'Why's that?'

Albert wriggled his lips. 'Because the thieves had to put them somewhere when they were stealing them. One cannot load two thousand Stiltons into the back of a car.' He explained his theory about the need for a specialist van. 'There cannot be that many places where a person can hire one. We might hit a dead end, we might get lucky, but it's worth looking into.'

'Yeah, sure,' said Oxford, wishing he'd thought of it first. 'You still want to go to the hospital, right?'

Albert nodded. 'Yes. For your investigation,' he was trying to make it all about Oxford so he would continue to help and because he hoped the boy might learn something, 'you need to know what the only witness to the robbery saw. He might be able to describe the van or truck. He might have seen the license plate. He might even be able to identify or describe the robbers.'

'Won't the chief inspector have got all that from him already?'

Oxford wasn't wrong. 'He will have, or certainly ought to have, but you're the one with local knowledge, Oxford.' Albert was buttering him up a bit. 'You might see a connection that no one else would. Do you know Dave Thornwell?'

'A bit, yeah. He was in my sister's year at school. He came to the house for parties a couple of times when they were teenagers. They never let me join in; I was just the bratty little brother, but I've seen him in the pub or about the village a few times since. He's got a really cute little sister. Well, she's twenty now, but I've always kept on his good side because ... well, you know.'

Albert ignored the young man's interest in the victim's sister and focussed on his local knowledge instead. 'There we go then. You already have the upper hand over the chief inspector.'

A broad smile surprised Oxford's face. 'Yeah, I suppose I do, don't I?' Then his brow creased. 'Do you think I will get in trouble for this?

Poking my nose into the CI's investigation, I mean?'

Albert didn't want to lie to the man. If he'd caught one of his junior officers conducting his own investigation into an ongoing case that was on his desk, he would've torn a strip off them and given them traffic duty for a year. That was him though and that was a different era. He settled on, 'Nothing ventured ...'

Oxford drove in silence for a while which gave Albert a chance to think. It was a huge amount of cheese to steal. Did the thieves have a buyer? Were they going straight out of the country? Would the chief inspector be wise enough to notify the ports? These questions and more besides popped up one after the other as he began to work out the logistics of stealing two thousand whole Stiltons. What about the timing of it? Was that important?

Rex sat on the back seat with one of the human seat belt things around him. He didn't know what it was supposed to do, but it wasn't bothering him, so he ignored it while he thought. They were going back the way they came earlier when they were in the taxi that smelled of cinnamon and nutmeg. He recognised the smells coming into the police car in reverse. Some of them were very familiar. There was the field which had recently been spread with poop – humans are so weird. Then they passed a dead fox, a roadside burger van, a field of sheep, and the list kept going all the way back to almost where they started. Rex closed his eyes and let his nose tell him where he was, only opening them again when they turned off the route in his head.

They were coming into a small city; he didn't need his eyes to tell him that. Nor did he require eyes to know when they arrived at a hospital.

He could see they were coming into a carpark though, and that meant he was going for a walk. Excited by the prospect because he hadn't had much exercise yet today, he bounced to his feet.

In the passenger seat, Albert turned his head to check out the dog. 'Try not to lick the windows, Rex, okay? You'll have to behave in here too. This is a hospital. Where they have lots of sick people.'

Rex rolled his eyes. His human was a nice old man, but sometimes he acted as if being a dog meant he was stupid.

Albert and Rex followed Oxford into the hospital's reception where the uniformed police officer had no problem attracting the attention of a lady behind the reception desk. It meant they skipped the line which Albert would otherwise have stood in for several minutes.

'I need to find a patient who was brought in a short while ago,' Oxford told the lady and gave her a friendly smile. 'His name is David Thornwell.'

The lady, a very tidy and trim woman in her forties, tapped the name into a computer. Her eyes flitted across the screen as she idly chewed her bottom lip. Albert noticed the trace of lipstick it left on her canine.

'He's in A&E,' she announced, then shifted her body to point the way.

'I guess I expected him to be in the accident and emergency ward still,' Oxford chattered away as they meandered through the hospital corridors. 'He'd been in the chiller for a few hours by the time they found him, but they said he was doing okay, and the cut to his head wasn't life threatening, I heard, so I suppose it won't need more than a couple of stitches so I doubt they will keep him in.'

Albert frowned. 'You didn't get to see him?'

Oxford snorted a laugh. 'Ha! The chief inspector doesn't like me. He doesn't like anyone much but he had me patrol the car park so no one would come near the cars. I didn't get to see anything. I only found out that it was Dave because Megan, that's one of the other officers, told me about it.'

Rex wasn't sure where they were going, but he could smell cheese again and couldn't work out why.

As they came into A&E, there was another reception desk manned by two more ladies, carbon copies of the ones in the main reception. Albert paused so Oxford could have them pinpoint Dave's location. There were lots of beds and many of them had curtains around them, but Oxford spotted the robbery victim the moment they came onto the ward and picked up his pace.

Albert almost got left behind as he paused by the reception desk, but Rex was following the new human they'd picked up today and tugged Albert's arm when he got to the end of his lead. Pulled off his feet so he stumbled, Albert hurried to catch up.

'Oh, hey, Oxford,' said the man on the bed. 'What are you doing here?' His head had been shaved at the back where a white dressing was stuck to his scalp. Dave Thornwell was twenty-two years old,

Albert decided, employing his years of describing suspects. Height and weight were difficult because he was in bed, but two hundred and twenty pounds and five feet ten, was Albert's best guess. The cheese thief victim was quite overweight, his belly stretched his hospital gown at the front and his chin tiered onto his chest with little discernible neck but he had a warm, if rueful, smile when Oxford approached his bed.

'Been in the wars?' Oxford joked. 'I'm here to ask you a few questions, of course. How are you feeling?'

With a shrug, Dave said, 'Oh, I'm fine. They said I was mildly dehydrated from being stuck in the chiller most of the night, and I needed three stitches in my head. Who's your friend?' Dave spotted the old man and his giant dog as they ambled up behind the cop and his forehead creased in question.

Oxford had momentarily forgotten his companions. 'This is um, this is Albert,' he had to scramble his brain to remember the name, 'and this is Rex.' He indicated the large dog who appeared to be cautiously sniffing Dave.

Dave stunk like cheese. Rex had never come across a person who stunk of anything as much as this guy stunk of Stilton. It was exactly the same smell that had overloaded him at the dairy earlier, only in a lesser volume and mixed in with some human smells.

Albert extended his hand. 'Pleased to meet you, young man. Oxford here has enlisted my help to catch the men that did this to you,' he announced.

'I have?' replied Oxford, sounding surprised.

'You're going to catch them?' echoed Dave, sounding equally surprised.

Albert answered them both at the same time. 'Yes.' Then to Oxford he said, 'I'm here for the festival, kid. It's the only reason for my visit. If that's not going ahead now, I have nothing better to do than help you solve this case. What do you say? I've got decades of experience investigating cases and a keen detective's mind. You've got youth and vitality, plus we've got Rex's nose. He was a police dog for a while and knows his stuff.' Albert left out the part where Rex got fired for having a bad attitude. 'We might only have until Saturday morning to find the cheese, but we could get lucky and, if nothing else, it will show your boss that you have enthusiasm and initiative.' He was laying it on thick, but none of what he said was necessarily wrong.

A smile broke out on Oxford's face. 'Yeah. We could solve the crime and catch the bad guys. That would make a splash at the station back in Peterborough. I'm fed up being the kid in Stilton who will never have to chase a real criminal.'

They both turned their attention to Dave on the bed. He looked quite panicked. 'What is it you need from me?' he blurted as if they were about to ask for a sample of his liver.

'Well,' said Albert, 'They locked you in the chiller. You must have got a look at them. That's what I heard the chief inspector say. I take it he didn't fully question you at the dairy.' Then, before he asked a proper question, Albert noticed what was amiss. 'Why isn't there a police officer with you already? Surely one must have accompanied you here.'

'It was Patrice,' Oxford supplied. 'The chief inspector sent her with you.' He looked around. 'Where is she?'

Dave said, 'She went to get herself a coffee. The doctor said I ought to stay here for a while so they could make sure I was okay. I feel fine though. Do you really think you can catch the man behind this?'

The question was clearly aimed at Albert, so he answered. 'The man? I got the impression it was a gang.'

'Yeah, yeah, that's what I meant,' said Dave. 'Yeah. I'm not sure exactly how many there were, of course.'

Albert looked about for a chair, spotted one at the next bed where the patient was asleep, and took it for himself. Once he was off his feet and his knees were taking a break, he said encouragingly, 'Why don't you tell us all about it. Start from the beginning and give us as much detail as possible.'

So that's what Dave did. 'My shift runs from six in the evening to six in the morning. I patrol the grounds and I watch the monitors. If I'm being honest, it's a slow and boring job, but it pays okay, and I can walk to work from my house. Plus, it's four days on and four days off.'

'Nevermind that,' Albert got in quick before he started listing other perks. 'How about the robbery, Dave. Tell us about that. What time was it when you first noticed or heard something?'

Dave looked at his watch, a response reaction to being asked a question that involved time. 'It was just after ten o'clock and I was performing one of my routine patrols when I heard a noise. I guess I knew instantly that something was wrong because I never hear anything at night; the village is the quietest place on Earth once the people go to bed. I should have called the police right there and then. Had I done so, I might have saved myself a lot of aggravation and several stitches but foolishly, I went to see what it could be.'

'What was it?' asked Oxford, his voice a hushed whisper.

'It was a truck backing up,' explained Dave.

Albert sighed; finally, they were getting somewhere. 'What sort of truck? Were there any recognisable marks on it? A brand or company logo? What colour? What make? Did you get a look at the number plate or maybe take a picture?' Albert nudged Oxford with his elbow. 'You should be taking notes of everything he says.'

'Right, yes, I should, shouldn't I?' The young police officer pulled a notebook and pen from his top left pocket.

Albert watched Dave's face as he considered his answer. 'It was an Iveco panel van, one of the temperature-controlled ones like we use at the dairy. I thought for a moment that it might be one of the dairy's trucks and I wandered over to it to see what was going on. It was backed up to the doors of the hâloir - that's the name of the room where cheese is left to mature,' he explained seeing the question form on Albert's face. 'I got about halfway there and realised that it wasn't one of our trucks at all. It was dark out, obviously, but they had the lights on inside the hâloir so they couldn't see me approaching but I could see them.'

'You saw them.' Albert grabbed onto that bit of information quickly. 'How many did you see?'

'Oh, err, well, I saw shadows. Their truck was backed up to the doors so I would have had to go down the side of the truck and into the hâloir in order to get a look at them, and by then they would be able to see me. There were at least three, but I think there might have been more than that.'

'Why do you say that?' Albert pressed him. All the details were important.

Dave looked like he was struggling for an answer. 'Um,' Now he looked truly flustered. 'Because they were talking, and it seemed like I could hear more than three voices.'

Albert considered what he was hearing for a second and backtracked a step. 'You saw the van and you think it was an Iveco panel van, the same as the dairy use. Was it old or new?'

Dave replied instantly. 'New.'

'What colour was it?'

'White.' Again, Dave's answer was confidently given. Albert drew a breath as he thought and huffed it out through his nose. He was becoming more confident of his concussion diagnosis. Complicated answers were confusing the poor boy, but simple yes/no, or one-word answers were easy.

Going with that strategy, he rephrased the next question in his head. 'You said you heard them talking, Dave. Did you hear what they were talking about? Yes or no is fine.'

'No. There was a breeze which was rustling the trees. I could hear them, but I couldn't make anything out,' Dave volunteered a load more information anyway. To Albert's surprise, Dave proved to be a decent witness, able to give answers clearly and concisely, and though he claimed to have seen nothing of worth, he provided enough detail to create a picture. As the questions went on, so Dave got more and more into the story. He was embellishing, which Albert knew from experience was quite normal. It was to be discouraged, but it was normal.

They went back and forth for ten minutes, as Albert slowly built up a picture of what happened. Dave worked at the dairy as a security guard and last night, at approximately ten o'clock, he discovered an unknown quantity of thieves robbing the cheese store. They were loading mature Stilton cheeses into a refrigerated truck, but he wasn't able to see their faces without giving himself away. He heard them speaking so was able to report that they spoke English with eastern European accents. Dave tried to call the police when it finally occurred to him to do so, but had no signal on his phone so rashly, he tried to steal the truck from the thieves. He got in and grabbed the steering wheel, but they hadn't left the keys in the ignition or anywhere in sight.

He jumped back down to go for help and that was when someone whacked him on the head. He woke up in the chiller a while later. Trapped in the dark, with no phone and no way out, he had to keep himself warm for the next seven hours until someone arrived and found him. Inexplicably, they also stole his shoes.

'That was quite a heroic thing to do,' Albert acknowledged duly. 'You were lucky to get away with just a bump on the head.'

Dave sort of half shrugged, acknowledging his bravery but not wanting anyone to dwell on it.

Albert wasn't finished with the interview yet though. 'What happened to your trousers?'

Dave's cheeks flushed. 'What do you mean?'

Albert was staring down at them. 'Only that you have mud splats on them.'

Dave looked down, his cheeks burning. 'Oh, goodness. So I do. They were clean on last night too. They knocked me out and stole my shoes, heaven knows why. I guess they must have dragged me through a puddle on the way to the chiller.'

Accepting his answer and moving on, Albert asked, 'You said they were talking to each other, Dave. Did any of them use names at any point?'

Dave's eyes widened as if stunned by the question. He'd been supplying more detail than Albert could have hoped for, but none of it was going to lead them to the thieves and the missing Stilton swiftly. What he really wanted was a name.

When Dave uncharacteristically failed to answer, Albert pressed him again. 'Come along, Dave. Thanks to you we know they were Eastern European. They were speaking to each other so at some point someone must have said a name. It might have been as a shout, when one person wanted to get the other person's attention.'

'Yeah!' Dave's eyes lit up. 'Yeah, sorry. I didn't think about it until now. One of them did shout a name. It was Karl. Karl something that ended with a Ski.'

'A ski?' Albert didn't follow.

'Yeah, you know, like Borski or Podlodowski or Zebrowski,' Dave tried to clarify.

'Karl Somethingski,' Oxford said as he wrote it down. 'That's really helpful, Dave. Thank you for your cooperation.' He swivelled around in his chair to look back down to the ward entrance. 'I wonder what happened to Patrice. She's been gone ages.'

Just then, the chief inspector wheeled around the corner with a young female police officer trailing him on either side.

Dave spotted him, then glanced at Albert and Oxford. 'Am I going to have to go through all that again with him?' he asked, clearly not relishing the concept.

Oxford pulled a sorry face. 'Probably, yes. Sorry.'

'Well, what was the point in me telling you all about it then?'

'What's going on here?' the chief inspector wanted to know as he approached Dave's bed. Oxford jumped to his feet. 'What are you doing here, Shaw? Why are you not in Stilton as you are supposed to be and why do you have this civilian with you?' He turned his eyes to look at Albert. 'You were at the dairy just an hour ago when I was there.'

'That's right,' said Albert. 'I was. I came over quite lightheaded and this young man,' he indicated Oxford, 'was good enough to bring me directly here.'

'You do not appear to be receiving treatment,' the chief inspector observed with accusing eyes.

'Yes. Thankfully, by the time we got here I felt much better. PC Shaw wanted me to get checked out but at my age I expect to have the odd funny turn every now and then. Since we were here anyway, PC Shaw wanted to check on his friend. You did know he was an acquaintance of the victim from the dairy, didn't you, Chief Inspector?'

Albert was deliberately dominating and manipulating the conversation so the chief inspector couldn't get a grip on it and so that Oxford wouldn't be able to say anything and put his foot in it.

Unfortunately, that didn't work because Oxford had bought Albert's line about getting himself noticed.

'Actually, sir, I thought I might be able to use my local knowledge to help crack the case. I was using my initiative and interviewing the witness swiftly while the information is still clear and fresh in his head.'

The chief inspector's eyes flared. 'By which you mean I have been dragging my feet by giving the injured man sufficient time to have his wound dressed.'

Oxford looked horrified. 'Oh, um, no, sir. That's not what I ...'

He got cut off before he could apologise. 'Tell me, Shaw. Since you appear to have taken this investigation from my desk and chosen to take it on yourself, what should your next steps be?'

Behind him, one of the two female officers snorted a small laugh at Oxford's expense. He was getting a proper reaming from the senior officer and Albert suspected he was only just gearing up to really lay into the young, inexperienced cop.

Withering under his gaze, Oxford gulped and tried to form a coherent answer. 'Well, sir, I guess I need to follow up on the leads the witness has provided and liaise with the crime scene guys to see what they were able to turn up. Then I will want to return to the scene to see if I can get a sense of ...' he tailed off to nothing as he realised he didn't have the faintest idea what he ought to do and the three cops staring at him knew it.

'Good luck then, Constable Shaw. I shall expect a full report when you have cracked the case. I'll let the dairy know they have nothing to worry about and can go ahead with the festival, shall I?'

Oxford's mouth had gone dry, but he managed to mumble, 'I'll do my best, sir.'

The chief inspector laughed in his face. 'You'll make a mess of the whole thing and embarrass yourself. The crime scene team will need at least forty-eight hours to make any sense of what they found so the festival was doomed from the moment the people behind this chose to steal the cheese. I'm sure they timed it because they knew there would be more in storage than normal. Can't stand the stuff myself. Go back to Stilton, Shaw. Stay there and try not to do anything stupid. My team will deal with this.' He finished speaking and glared at Oxford, who couldn't work out where to look. Impatiently, the chief inspector snapped, 'Get out of the way, Shaw! I need to speak to Mr Thornwell.'

'Yes, sir. Sorry, sir.' Shaw grabbed his hat and his notepad as fast as he could, almost falling over in his haste to get out of the senior officer's way.

Albert didn't bother to move and nor did Rex, who was aware there was tension between some of the humans but had no interest in their squabbling. Oxford was standing a few feet away, jerking his head and doing what he could to catch Albert's eye. He wanted to do as the chief inspector expected and return to Stilton. He was in enough trouble already without now hanging around. If the old man didn't move soon, he was going to have to leave without him.

Then he remembered the old man's suitcase and backpack were in the boot of his squad car.

'Mr Thornwell,' the chief inspector addressed the man on the bed with a kindly tone. 'I apologise for that unfortunate display. I'm afraid my junior officer rather overstepped his bounds. I've no wish to trouble you any further at this time. I will need to interview you, but there is no rush. Unless you feel up to being interviewed right now?' he asked the question in such a way that it was obvious he wanted Dave to say no.

'I just told Oxford everything I know,' he complained.

The chief inspector's head snapped around to glare at PC Shaw once more, but he held back on yet another reprimand. When he looked back at Dave, his soothing tone was still in place. 'That's unfortunate, Mr Thornwell, because that interview will not count. I must ask that you come by the station once you are recovered. Any time in the next twenty-four hours, please.'

Albert couldn't help the deep frown from forming on his forehead. 'Any time in the next twenty-four hours? Criminals just got away with hundreds of thousands of pounds worth of goods and you are happy to wait a day before even interviewing the only witness?'

With a sniff of annoyance, the chief inspector turned his gaze on Albert. 'This crime will not be solved in time for the festival, sir, if at all. As I explained to Mr Brenner, there will always be far more serious crimes to pursue than some missing cheese. It will get the attention it deserves but I will not be cajoled into prioritising it over a double homicide.'

'You have a double homicide?' Albert was surprised to hear it. This region of the country was so quiet and peaceful. It was a rural area. But, of course, murder can happen anywhere, as he well knew.

He didn't get an answer to his question though. The chief inspector simply glared passively and held his gaze as he got to his feet. Once he was upright, he broke it off so he could address the dairy's security guard. 'Mr Thornwell, within twenty-four hours, please.' He didn't wait for a reply, and with the two female officers falling in behind him again, he offered one final sneer at Oxford. 'Get back to Stilton and stay there.'

The air felt heavy when the chief inspector finally left; Albert, Dave, and Oxford all just looked at each other for a second. However, it wasn't long before Albert's face split into a broad grin. 'He was fun,' he chuckled. 'I've met a few tightly wound people in my life, but he is challenging for the top spot.' Using his hands to push off his knees and help him get upright, he struggled back to his aging feet. 'I expect his head will simply implode when he hears you have solved this and returned the cheese in time for the festival.'

Oxford stared at the old man in bewilderment. 'He just chewed my butt off for speaking to his witness.'

'He also challenged you to solve the case,' Albert countered.

Oxford's brow creased as he reran the conversation in his head. 'I don't remember him challenging me to solve it.'

Dave chipped in too, 'Yeah, I don't remember that either.'

Albert chuckled lightly. 'It was subtextual. He gave you a direct order to get back to Stilton and he asked you to consider what your next move should be. You have an office in Stilton?'

'Yeah. There's a whole cottage for the senior resident policeman. It has a dedicated office on one side.' Oxford's left leg was twitching to get to the car. He had an awful feeling the CI was about to reappear and really go at him because he still hadn't left.

'The office has a computer, right?' Albert asked, knowing the answer in advance. 'You can do mug shots and cross checks and things like that, can't you?'

'Yeah.' Oxford wasn't sure he liked where this was going.

Albert shot Dave a quick wave goodbye and started back toward the exit from the ward. 'Constable Shaw, I think it's time you did some police work.'

Police Work

'Karl Somethingski cannot be a popular name. I bet if he is stealing a huge amount of cheese, he will have a rap sheet. We just need to interrogate your clever keyboard and see what it spits out. Maybe we'll get lucky.' Oxford was finding it hard to weather the perpetual storm of Albert's positive attitude. He had to give the old man a lift back to Stilton and on the way, Albert talked the whole time about solving crimes and taking down criminals. It was the stuff Oxford joined up to do. He dreamed of hand-to-hand combat to subdue a crazed knife-wielding gangster, and driving his car through the village at more than twice the speed limit in pursuit of a killer attempting to flee justice. Those were his fantasies. In reality, he hadn't even made his first arrest and was yet to find a legitimate reason to switch on his squad car's roof lights and siren.

The office in Stilton was in fact a house. Or rather, it was a pretty little cottage with a central door at the end of a garden path. Even though it was autumn, and the leaves were gone from the trees, there were plenty of evergreen shrubs planted to give the garden some colour. Albert had seen a few of these cottages before when he still served.

Remote rural communities had a local bobby and he needed a place to work, so they converted a house, or more likely, when community police officers first came into existence, a house was built to accommodate them. This was one of those and it looked to be a hundred and fifty years old or more.

Oxford parked in front of the house, but he didn't go down the path to the door, he went around the side of the house to a different door. It still had an old blue police light mounted above it. Albert stared at it in fascination; he hadn't seen one in years.

'Does that thing still work?' he asked, staring up at it.

Oxford laughed out loud. 'Yeah. If you put a candle in it. This place might have a computer and a phone, but that's about the only updates they've given Stilton in the last century. The light isn't even wired in.'

The door on the side of the house led into the local police officer's office. There was a door leading from it to the rest of the house, but Albert was sure he would find the door to be locked from the other side if he checked. 'You said the senior officer for Stilton just retired?' he queried.

'Mark? Yeah, the new guy starts on Monday. Even though it's the festival this weekend, they didn't think it mattered if he wasn't here and they are sending additional officers from Peterborough to cover the event.' Oxford settled himself in front of the computer and booted it into life. There were passwords to enter and suchlike, but once he was in, it was a simple process to interrogate the system for known criminals with the first name Karl and a last name ending in Ski.

Albert smiled to himself that he didn't have to call one of his children for help this time.

'Wow,' whispered Oxford mostly to himself. Out of the chief inspector's sphere of influence, he'd allowed himself to fantasise about actually solving the case, but of course his simple search for a likely suspect returned over two thousand possibilities. That was that then.

Albert wasn't confident with computers. It took him many hours with a surprisingly patient nine-year-old granddaughter to get anywhere near to competent with his phone; a computer was just a step too far. Randall, his youngest son, would always want to show Albert the things his computer could do as if that were going to change his mind, and he'd seen Gary use the system at work to find information in a heartbeat so he knew how good the police intranet was. Nevertheless, looking over Oxford's shoulder, he saw the number of matches displayed on the screen and pursed his lips as he accepted that modern technology couldn't do everything.

'Hold on, Oxford. How wide did you cast your net?'

Oxford swung his head around to look at the old man. 'What do you mean?'

'Well you have two thousand possible matches, but the population of Stilton isn't much more than that.'

Oxford gave himself a mental head slap and moved the mouse. He'd left it set to national, so he'd just searched the entire country for matches. If they had any chance of getting a result with this case, the Karl they were looking for had to be local. Or at least within a few miles. Zeroing in on Stilton, he clicked the search button again and this time got no matches. He expanded by a mile and still got no hits. Another mile and another click of the mouse and the computer returned a result containing one match.

Karl Tarkovsky, a forty-eight-year-old lifelong criminal. Originally from Lithuania, Karl had been found guilty of assault, affray, sexual assault and seven counts of either burglary or robbery. He'd spent a total of four years in jail across eight different incarcerations and his mugshot showed an ugly guy with terrible tattoos that ran up his neck and onto his head. His nose was skewed to one side like a boxer who'd seen far too many bouts and a chunk was missing out of his right ear like an alley cat. He wasn't showing any teeth in the picture, but Albert was willing to bet some of them were missing. He looked like a person who wanted to start a fight.

The humans were busy messing about at the desk, which left Rex to explore. He was feeling in need of a snack. To be fair, his default setting was that he was in need of a snack, but breakfast had become a distant memory and he could smell food. To start with, there was a pizza box giving off enticing smells from the bin in the corner. The bin was three feet high and had a flip top lid. He could get into it to explore the pizza box and other treats easily enough, however, he couldn't do it without his human noticing, and he would instantly disapprove. Chances were it didn't have any food in it anyway. The problem with pizza boxes was the grease dripped into the cardboard and stayed there, giving a disproportionate amount of smell long after the food had gone.

His nose led him around the kitchen to his next target. There was a jar of coffee and a box of teabags on the side next to some mismatched mugs. He could smell the coffee when he came in, but it held no interest for him. The pack of Hobnob biscuits however were exactly what he wanted to find and though he'd picked up the scent when the door opened, he hadn't expected to find them open and spilled out on the side.

Rex checked over his shoulder, just in case his human, or the other one for that matter, were looking, but they were both absorbed in what they were doing. Deftly snagging the first delicious round morsel, he crunched it as quietly as he could, which wasn't very quiet, truth be told – dog mouths are not meant for surreptitious eating. He got away with it, so risked a second, and then a third.

'I'll take those, thank you, Rex.' Albert's hand darted in to pluck the packet just as Rex grabbed the fourth and fifth sweet treat. Rex didn't care by then; it wasn't like his human could make him give them back now he'd eaten them.

Albert stomped back to the desk with the computer. 'Honestly, you'd think I didn't feed him.' The obvious rustling noise of the biscuit wrapper took a moment to penetrate Albert's brain because he'd been so focussed on what they'd found. Oxford was still reading it now, flicking between pages as he used Karl's details to add yet more information.

Karl had known associates – all Lithuanian – as if it were a gang, but they didn't look that organised, and if their records were anything to go by, they weren't particularly competent either. That he had friends who were also bungling crooks was interesting but there were other details that jumped off the page. He had an address in nearby Washingley.

Oxford found that he was chewing his knuckles. He wasn't used to making decisions. When he woke up this morning, he expected another quiet day of doing not very much. Saturday would prove testing because the festival would attract lots of people and that meant petty theft, double parking, public drunkenness, and a dozen other insignificant misdemeanours. The cops from Peterborough would most likely take over and deal with anything interesting. Oxford expected to be given a rubbish job like directing traffic so the main route through the town wouldn't get snarled up and blocked. Nothing interesting was ever going to happen in Stilton. At least that was what he had always believed.

Until this morning. Suddenly, this morning there was a major robbery, which ought to have been exciting but no sooner than he got to the scene than he had to accept it was too big for him. Dutifully, he'd called it in and within half an hour had a chief inspector directing him to manage the carpark. Now he had the address for a criminal who the sole witness identified as being at the scene. He could get in his squad car, go to the man's address, and arrest him.

It was a terrifying proposition. Not because Karl Tarkovsky looked like a thug, that didn't make him nervous, it was the responsibility of taking that step that had him feeling trepidatious. What would the chief inspector say?

Albert could see the young man's internal tussle and tried to remember what it had been like for him when he was so young and new. Junior officers don't get to do much by themselves ever, they are umbilically attached to a more experienced officer. Albert saw the truth of it: he'd been pressing Oxford to go after the bad guys who stole the cheese and the poor kid just wasn't ready.

He placed a hand on Oxford's shoulder. 'I think maybe we should stop now. The right thing would be to make sure the chief inspector or someone close to him has this information and then focus on dealing with the minor quandaries that occur here in Stilton.'

Oxford slumped back into his chair. That sounded like a good idea, but when he wanted to agree, he found that he couldn't, and he shook his head. 'No. No, I think I should go to his address at least. It's not far away and the CI said I was to deal with problems in Stilton – this is a Stilton problem.' With his jaw set, he pushed back his chair and stood up. His boldness lasted only a few seconds though. 'Um, would you like to come for a ride along?'

Albert had to chuckle. 'Sure, kid. That sounds fun.'

Karl Tarkovsky

T he address took them to a house on Mung Lane in the small village of Washingley. It was about one third of the size of Stilton and therefore wasn't really a village at all. It was more of a hamlet – a collection of dwellings clustered together with a pub and a church to make things interesting on a Friday night and a Sunday morning.

The house was a rundown terrace place with paint flaking off the stonework above the windows and doors where someone, possibly a former owner, had chosen to highlight the period features. The drainpipe was broken and had been for some time if the water stain running down the wall was anything to go by. Parts of a motorbike lay forgotten in a pile under the one ground floor window in a stain of old oil. Weeds grew rampant wherever they could.

'A Fastidious homeowner,' Albert noted to himself as he took it all in.

Oxford had driven directly to the house and would have parked in front of it had Albert not spoken. 'You should park down the road.

Just far enough out of sight that anyone watching from inside doesn't automatically assume you are there for them.'

Oxford nodded. 'You think he might bolt?'

Albert pursed his lips. 'I doubt he is there, truthfully. If he stole two hundred grand's worth of cheese last night, he is most likely on his way to deliver it to the buyer or has already done so. But we might get lucky. Perhaps the task is done, and he is back home counting his share of the takings.'

'Let's hope so,' said Oxford. 'Two hundred grand. That sounds like a lot of money, but I guess that's the retail value. No one will pay that for stolen goods and then he has to split what they do get with the rest of the crew. It doesn't sound like much when you're risking another spell in jail.'

Perplexed at the maths, Albert hadn't thought about it in those terms. Oxford was right though; it wasn't a lot of money to make. There had to be higher value targets around. 'You can ask him about it when we catch up to him. I'm going to go around the back. If he decides to scarper when you knock on the door, he'll come out the back and Rex will corner him.'

'He can do that?' Oxford looked at the dog dribbling on the backseat.

Albert opened his door and put one foot out. 'Like I said before; he used to be a police dog. Getting him to corner Karl won't be a problem. Stopping him from eating him might be.'

'Sorry, Albert, I can't allow that. This is a police matter. It would be gross negligence on my part if I were to involve you in the attempted apprehension of a suspect.'

Duly informed, Albert suggested he busy himself in another way. 'I'll just take Rex for a walk then. He could do with stretching his legs.'

Relieved that the old man hadn't tried to fight him, Oxford set off toward the doors. 'Please do that. Like you said: chances are that he will not be here.'

Albert watched PC Shaw approach the house over one shoulder as he looked about for an alleyway that would get him behind the houses. All terraced houses had them; narrow paths that led behind or between the rows of houses as if someone a long time ago decided that was how the design should be and everyone then copied.

The alleyway was badly overgrown. In the summer it would be impassable, but summer was long gone and with it most of the foliage, so only the hardier stems and branches remained. Rex shoved through them as if they weren't there, keen to get wherever they were going, and had to wait as Albert ducked and swerved and wondered if he was going to get trapped. Pushing through a final pair of branches, the alleyway opened out onto a potholed back road that ran behind the houses. There were garages opposite for owners to park their cars and room for cars to be parked between or in the potholes. Edging around puddles that looked big enough to take a bath in, Albert counted off the houses and found a garden gate.

At the front door, Oxford knocked politely. He didn't want to tip his hand, so chose to not announce loudly it was the police at the door. Perhaps Karl would be inside watching afternoon soap operas and come to the door to see who it was. Oxford's polite knocking got no response though, so he tried again with more volume and purpose. The result returned was unchanged from his first attempt, so he switched to insistent hammering and declared, 'Police. Open up.'

In the back garden, because the gate leading from the back road onto the property 'accidentally' came open when Albert put his hand over the top and undid the bolt holding it closed, Rex and his human waited for something to happen. It was quiet out in the countryside, no sound at all apart from chirping birds and the drone of a tractor somewhere far in the distance so both man and dog heard when Oxford yelled his presence and thumped on the door.

Telling himself to be ready, Albert watched the back door. If Oxford spooked Karl and he ran, Albert didn't want to get knocked over and hurt. Nothing happened though, and it was much as he expected. The day after pulling off a violent robbery, the criminal wasn't sitting in his house, he was delivering the stolen wares and getting paid. Unfortunately, that meant the trail had gone cold for the time being and they didn't have the time to wait for Karl to return home.

His internal debate about whether he ought to 'accidentally' go inside the house lasted about four seconds, but he did use a handkerchief on his right hand when he touched the back door to check if it was unlocked.

'Well, what do you know?' he asked the air as the door swung inwards.

Rex looked up at his human. 'What are we doing? Are we going in?'

Albert looked down at Rex, meeting his gaze and getting the impression the dog was asking a question. He chose to explain their predicament. 'The problem as I see it, Rex, is that technically, if I go in it will be breaking and entering. Young Oxford cannot go in at all because he has no warrant and no probable cause to enter the premises without the homeowner's permission. However, and here is where we meet a small and quite tenuous loophole, if my dog were to tug at his lead, my old gnarled fingers might just not be able to keep hold of him.' Albert nudged Rex's bum with his left foot, causing the dog to get up suddenly. 'Oh, look at that! My dog surged ahead and got away from me. Now, if said dog were to run into the house, I wouldn't be able to stop him.'

Rex stared up at his human, wondering what the idiot was babbling on about. There were too many words and he was getting confused. Rex liked simple commands: Sit, stay, heel, bite the man who is running away. Was he supposed to go into the house or not?

'Go,' insisted Albert.

Rex raised his eyebrows in question. Now it seemed like his human wanted to play a game. He bounced around on his paws, ready for whatever game this was. Did his human have a ball? He loved a ball to chase. Or a frisbee! Frisbees were the best.

'Go!' urged Albert. The damned dog always did whatever Albert didn't want him to do so it was typical now that he chose to refuse to go in the house.

On the other side of the property, Oxford hammered one last time. The suspect either wasn't at home or had gone out the back and escaped. There was nothing he could do about it, but just as he was about to walk away, he saw a shadow shift inside. Through the small, head-height, frosted glass panel, someone was moving deep inside the house and as he held his breath, it became obvious the indistinct form was coming his way.

A security chain came off, and a bolt slid along its barrel at the bottom of the door. Oxford licked his lips and got ready to face the imposing form of Karl Tarkovsky.

'Ooh, me back,' moaned a voice on the other side of the door. It made Oxford's right eyebrow raise all by itself and the fear he felt for what he might see next came true when the door swung open to show Albert inside the house. 'Oh, lad, it's a long way down to those floor bolts at my age.'

Albert had a handkerchief over his fingers which he held in place with his other hand so he could touch things without leaving his fingerprints. That didn't change anything though and Oxford's face became thunder.

'You just broke into a house, Albert!' he growled.

'No, I didn't,' Albert said while doing his best to look shocked at the accusation. In truth, he was trying to suppress a cheeky grin. 'Rex got away from me, lad. You don't know what it's like to get old. My hand strength isn't what it was, and the back door was open. I think he must have smelled food because he was in the house like a weasel up a trouser leg. I had to come in to get him because he wouldn't come out.'

Narrowing his eyes at the blatant lie, Oxford maintained his insistent tone. 'You can leave now, Albert.'

'I haven't found the dog yet.'

'Rex!' Oxford tried calling the dog.

Albert joined in. 'Rex! Here, Rex. Come on, boy!' whistles, calls, and encouragement failed to make the dog return to the front door. 'Maybe we should go and look for him,' suggested Albert.

With an angry sigh, Oxford glared at the old man. 'I cannot enter the property and you know it. I have no warrant and no probable cause to think there is danger to life.'

'Righto. I'll just see if I can find him then.' Albert ducked back inside the house, leaving the front door ajar as he went back upstairs to where he'd tied Rex's lead to a door handle.

Rex gave his human a single tail wag as his head reappeared around the edge of the stairs. He wasn't sure what they were up to, not that he often understood human activity; they always seemed to be ludicrously busy, but there was a new house to explore and that meant all manner of fun smells and possibly some food.

At the top of the stairs, Albert unhooked Rex's lead, then lowered himself gingerly to the floor, got comfortable and whacked the carpet as hard as he could with his right hand. The move was accompanied by a cry for help. 'Arrrgh! Arrrgh!' unable to suppress his mirth any longer, he chuckled to himself. 'There's your probable cause, lad.'

Tapping his foot impatiently, Oxford heard the thump and the cries of pain that followed. He exploded into action, shouldering the door aside as he burst through it. 'Albert! Albert call out! Where are you?'

Sniggering still, Albert put on a pathetic wounded voice. 'I'm upstairs, lad.'

Fast feet, stomping heavily up the stairs in copper's boots arrived just as Albert was levering himself off the floor. He felt ready for an Oscar-worthy performance, but he just couldn't keep his face straight. Looking up at Oxford's concern, he saw the young man's expression switch to one of disbelief and annoyance.

'Albert,' Oxford growled through gritted teeth. 'This is not cool.'

Dropping his pretence, Albert clambered to his feet using the top of the banister for leverage. 'Oh well, you're in here now. I guess we ought to have a quick look around, don't you?'

'No, Albert. I think we ought to vacate the premises immediately, before the owner comes home or someone else catches us. Pretending to be hurt is not probable cause to enter a house.'

'Aha!' Albert held up an index finger. 'That's where you'd be wrong, me ladio. You couldn't tell what my condition might be, so you did have probable cause to invade the home. If it ever came to court, which it won't, you could defend your actions. It is I who cannot defend mine. Anyway, enough jibber jabber. The back door was open, and the resident is a known criminal suspected of being involved in a violent robbery in the last twenty-four hours. I think we need to perform a visual search on our way out. He could be lying dead in one of the bedrooms for all we know.' Albert knew he wasn't because Rex would be going nuts if he were.

Feeling defeated, accepting Albert was right, and knowing he wasn't going to get the old man out without arresting him, Oxford threw his arms in the air in frustration. 'Alright. Quickly though. And don't touch anything.'

They did a cursory search. There were two bedrooms; one at the front of the house and one at the back plus a tiny bathroom. One bedroom, the slightly larger one, was neat and tidy. Things were put away and a pot of scented wood shavings gave the room a pleasant lavender smell. The other room was a tip and it was clear the scruffy room belonged to Karl Tarkovsky because there were Lithuanian language magazines on the carpet.

Oxford was mostly trying to get Albert to give up and leave the house. Don't touch anything fell on deaf ears as Albert opened a closet in Karl's bedroom.

'Does it look like something used to be here, but isn't here anymore?' Albert asked. Inside, the closet was stuffed full. On every shelf to the left and right were items of clothing stuffed in roughly so the shelves contained about double what they could comfortably hold. The rail positioned just above head height was bowing dangerously in the middle from all the clothing hanging from it, and the floor was littered with shoes and items of clothing which had fallen from the shelves. Most of it was new, that was the first thing Albert noticed. There were older items, but those were the ones stuffed haphazardly onto the shelves.

Albert backed up a pace and looked around until he spotted a wastepaper basket. He didn't touch it, but looking inside, he found tags torn from new clothes. 'He's recently come into some money,' he said more to himself than to Oxford.

The young man heard though and joined him in looking in the wastepaper basket. 'There are six new shoeboxes by his bed. They are all designer brand and must be worth at least five hundred pounds. Maybe double that.'

The clothes and shoes indicated a spending spree, but right in the middle of the closet, where everything around was chaos and disorder, was a three-foot by three-foot space. There were indentations in the carpet to show that something heavy had been resting there until quite recently and it looked like a pair of matching suitcases.

Oxford leaned in to look and though he wanted to leave, he couldn't help himself from questioning what he was now looking at. It looked like Karl had packed and left. 'Do you think maybe he took the Stiltons to Lithuania?'

Albert didn't get a chance to answer.

Intruder Alert

Rex had taken himself downstairs. There were no interesting smells upstairs save for those coming from the laundry hamper which contained soiled underpants and sweaty clothes that were now several days old and reaching a mature level of stench. The man's bedding was ripe too. His human sent him from the room when he tried to get the laundry hamper open, so he was downstairs where the kitchen seemed likely to yield something worth eating.

With his front paws on the counter, he sniffed along to the breadbin. There was definitely something inside, but how to open it? Pondering one of life's great questions – how to get to the food. The man at the window caught him completely by surprise.

The eruption of barking reached Albert's ears and he knew the dog well enough to be able to tell the difference between his barks. This was not an excited bark because he'd spotted a cat or a squirrel. It was the bark he used when he was going to bite someone.

'Quick, man!' he yelled at Oxford. 'He's got someone!' Albert knew he'd most likely pop a hip if he tried to run down the stairs and he knew Rex would bite without thinking if he thought the threat was real.

Oxford had no idea what was going on. One moment, they were staring at some indentations in the carpet of a closet in a room they shouldn't be in, in a house the old man had broken into. The next, the dog was going nuts downstairs and the old man was shouting and slapping him on the arm to get him moving.

Reacting instinctively, Oxford ran from the room. The old man was following, but at his speed, the dog would have eaten whoever was there before Albert got down the stairs. Oxford leapt from top to bottom, tucking into a roll as he hit the carpet to bounce up onto his feet again. With a kick off the wall to arrest his motion and convert it into speed going the other way, he shot through the house toward the back door.

Albert saw Oxford's gymnastic display and marvelled at today's youth. He couldn't have done that at his most flexible or fittest. Then again, the word Parkour hadn't been invented sixty years ago. Shuffling down the stairs as fast as he could go, he could still hear Rex barking. It meant he didn't have a mouthful of arm or leg or, heaven forbid, something squishier.

Oxford sprinted through the house praying the dog hadn't maimed Karl Tarkovsky. The owner arriving home and getting mauled would really put the shine on his illegal entry and search. He'd be lucky to keep his job. The incessant barking was coming from outside which surprised Oxford because he'd made a point of checking the back door was shut earlier. It was open now, that was for sure, and running for it, he caught sight of the dog's back end and tail as he pranced around and leapt in the air.

Bursting from the house into the grey autumn daylight outside, he found the dog still going nuts, and a man clinging to a tree branch for dear life. The back of the man's jacket was ripped where Rex had got his teeth into it as the man hung upside down and perilously within biting distance. However, even looking at his panic-stricken face side on, Oxford could tell it wasn't Karl Tarkovsky.

'Call it off!' the man begged fearfully. 'Call it off, this is my house!'

PC Shaw tried to grab hold of the excited dog, but Rex had to weigh almost the same as he did and was probably stronger. 'Down, Rex!' he commanded. 'Down!'

Rex leapt into the air again. He'd heard the new human's instructions but didn't feel like they needed to apply to his new game. He wasn't going to hurt the human in the tree, but he liked how scared he smelled.

Somewhat out of breath and leaning on the doorframe for support, Albert put two fingers in his mouth and whistled. 'Enough, Rex!' His bellow followed the eardrum-piercing whistle and stopped the giant dog before he could take his next leap.

Disappointed the game was over, Rex sat his hind quarters down and let his tail wag lazily. Until the man tried to move, that is. Then he curled his top lip and gave him a growl just to see what he would do.

The man in the tree had been gingerly taking one foot down to get it back to the ground. He couldn't hold on much longer, and the dog still wasn't under control. However, trying to get his foot back up to the branch didn't work. He wasn't fit enough to keep holding on and the initial burst of adrenalin induced effort to get into the tree was now spent. As his leg flailed, he lost his grip and tumbled from the tree. It was only a distance of about seven feet, but it was still going to hurt.

Mercifully, for all involved, Oxford saw the man was going to fall and darted forward, catching him with both arms like a baby before popping him down, right way up, on his feet.

'Keep him back!' the man wailed, using Oxford as a barrier between his body and the dog. Rex's interest in the man had already waned and he wandered off to sniff the undergrowth while the humans talked.

Albert ambled across the small patch of overgrown lawn to clip Rex back onto his lead. Hazarding a guess, he said, 'Are you the homeowner, sir?'

Now that the beast of a dog was on his lead and no longer looking threatening, the man managed to look indignant. 'Yes, I jolly well am. This is my house and I would like to know what you are doing in it.'

'Your name, sir?' asked Oxford with a resigned sigh; he was going to get skinned by the chief inspector when he found out.

'Donald Chessman.' Donald still looked haughty, but under Albert's silent gaze, he folded like a cheap deckchair. 'Is this to do with Karl?'

Albert gave the man a slow nod. 'Would you like to invite us inside for a cup of tea so the neighbours don't hear all about it?' he suggested. Several curtains had twitched in the last thirty seconds, as people either side and farther along the street poked their faces out to see what might be causing the hullabaloo.

Wearily, Donald nodded. 'Is the dog safe to be around?' He was taking his jacket off; a cheap, fake leather thing that was now worthless unless mauled by a dog was all the rage as a look this year.

'Sorry about that,' Albert apologised. 'He was most likely startled by your arrival home.'

Holding his jacket up to inspect it, Donald looked suitably irked, but managed to be stoical instead of angry. 'At least he didn't get me. I have to tell you,' he admitted with a snort as he led them back inside, 'seeing the dog the other side of the back door when I opened it is the scariest thing I have ever seen.'

Some Truth

O xford did the duty with the kettle, scaring up some clean cups as Donald jabbered continuously at what passed for a dining table. There were only two chairs, so he was going to have to stand, but that was okay, the chairs were mismatched and looked like they might fall apart if one of the men suddenly sneezed.

'It's my wife, you see. Or the lawyers, I suppose, depending on one's opinion. She cheated on me and left me, but somehow she gets the house and I have to pay all the bills and hand over all my savings just because she gets to keep the kids. I could have kept the kids,' he moaned. 'But they wanted to stay with mum because mum has always been there for them. Why wasn't I there? Because I was out earning a living so she could stay at home on her ever-widening bum looking after the kids. They left me penniless, but it gets worse.' He wagged a knowing finger.

Oxford used the lull in his rant to hand him a steaming mug of tea.

'The man she was cheating with then moves into my house and sleeps in my bed. My bed! He doesn't even have a job so his earnings do not form a contribution and he's there all the time so the kids already love him more than me. This cruddy place was all I could afford to buy, and I can't afford to do anything to fix it up. I had to take on a lodger just so I had enough money to feed myself. I asked him to move out when I got the impression he was a bit of a criminal or something. He was always appearing with boxes of dodgy gear. He tried to pay me in cigarettes once. He told me they were as good as cash, but what I am supposed to do with cigarettes? They were either stolen or illegally imported so with my luck I'd get arrested if I tried to sell them on. Anyway, he refused to move out and doesn't bother to pay me any rent anymore. He thinks I'm a joke, just like my wife.' Donald was somewhere in his late forties or early fifties. A Caucasian man with a pot belly and a receding hairline. Shorter than average at around five feet seven inches tall, he didn't have much going for him in the looks department and gave off a depressing vibe as he carried around that which had happened to him like a medal to show people.

Albert worried that the man might start sobbing but soon realised he was too angry for that. Donald was as likely to go berserk on a revenge-fuelled shotgun spree as any man he'd ever met.

'Do you own a shotgun?' Albert asked.

Donald's eyebrows rose to the top of his skull. 'No, why?'

'No reason.' Albert quickly ended that line on enquiry and moved onto the next. 'What did Karl do for a living?'

Oxford wasn't happy that they were interviewing the man, but he had invited them in and didn't seem at all unhappy that they had been in his house. In fact, he got the impression Donald was thankful for it and wanted them to help him get rid of his unwanted houseguest.

Donald's instant reply was, 'I don't think he does anything legal. I mean, he always had money, but I don't think he ever went to a job. He did claim some kind of disability benefit, not that I think there was anything wrong with him, but he was getting money from the system because I accidentally opened a letter that came for him thinking it was another letter from my wife's lawyers.'

Conscious that the old man had been directing his actions, steering him along and asking all the questions, Oxford felt it was time he got involved and he had a question to ask. 'Did he ever mention Stilton, Mr Chessman? The cheese that is, not the village. Though, I suppose talking about the village might also be of interest.'

'Stilton?' Donald echoed. 'I don't think so. Karl and I didn't exactly talk. Mostly, I avoided him and spent my evenings hiding in my room. He often had friends come over and it was quite clear I wasn't invited to join in.'

Albert was beginning to feel quite sorry for the man. 'Does he own a car? Did you ever hear him talking about a big job that he might have coming up?'

'A car? Yes. It's a black BMW five series. An old one from the nineties. It's usually outside.'

Oxford went to look, and the conversation paused for a moment. Donald and Albert both took a gulp of tea while they waited for the younger man to return.

'It's still there,' PC Shaw announced. The road outside was almost devoid of cars, which made the 1994 plate black BMW stand out. He'd taken a picture of the licence plate in case it came in handy later.

The car hadn't gone, but Karl had, and it looked like he'd taken two suitcases with him. In Albert's head he could picture the Lithuanian stealing the cheese with the belief that he could sell it for a decent amount at home. He'd then absconded the moment it was all loaded inside, taking his friends, the cheese, and any hope of catching him in the process. It was a tough blow for the festival and probably spelled the end of his investigation. It had been fun for a couple of hours, but then Donald said something that reignited it in glorious fashion.

'I assume you already know he owns a small lock up.'

What's Inside Door Number Five?

The news jolted Albert from his bored acceptance that the case and the festival were in the can and gave him a new place to look. 'A lock up, you say?'

'Yeah. There's a key for it hanging up by the door. You could check it out,' Donald suggested hopefully. 'Maybe there's a whole load of stolen things in it. I sure would appreciate it if you could send him back to jail.' Donald was all but pleading.

'I would need a warrant to be able to conduct a search,' Oxford had no intention of falling for any more of Albert's sneaky tricks.

'But there's nothing to stop Donald from using the key to open the lockup,' argued Albert. 'It is legitimately available for him to use because it is in his property.'

Oxford hung his head. He was going to get busted and he just didn't know how to avoid it. 'That's not how it works, Albert.'

Albert grinned. 'But who's to say?'

The lockup was at the end of Fen Lane which lay at the eastern extreme of the village and close to the A1(M) motorway. To get to it, they had to follow the country lanes back to Stilton and cross through it.

'Hey, there's Dave Thornwell,' said Oxford, pointing through the squad car's windscreen. It was supposed to have just him in it, but was beginning to feel like a taxi. Donald was riding shotgun in the passenger seat now that Albert had moved into the back to sit with Rex. The old man had the dog's head on his lap and his arm around the animal's shoulders. They came across as a content and well-synched pairing, as if each supported the other in a way that they couldn't manage by themselves. Oxford saw Albert look up and peer through the windscreen, so he pointed again.

Albert's short-range vision was terrible, but long distance, he had eyes like a hawk and sure enough it was Dave Thornwell. He had a beanie hat on to cover the dressing on the back of his head, and he was walking away from them, but due to his size and shape, he was easy to spot.

Oxford swung the squad car across the street, crossing lanes to get to the other side, where he pulled to stop just feet behind the dairy's security guard. 'Dave!'

Dave stopped moving as if someone had noisily chambered a round and told him to freeze.

Oxford called his name again. 'Dave?' Only this time when he said it, it came out as a question.

Dave turned slowly, coming to face the car, and only then fixing his face so it was smiling. 'Hi, Oxford,' he tried. 'What's going on?'

'Your statement, Dave. We might have found where the Stilton is hidden already. We're on our way to a lockup on Fen Lane. Jump in.'

'Jump in?' Dave echoed, looking shocked at the concept. Albert was having trouble reading Dave's expression, but analysing his face, he considered that he would need to find an unexpected pineapple in his pants to achieve the same look – the man looked terrified.

Oxford was brimming with enthusiasm. 'Yeah. You never know, it might be that they haven't shifted it yet and the cheese is still there. You could save the day. I bet the dairy would give you a bonus or something for recovering the cheese.'

Dave shifted his feet uncomfortably, but said, 'Sure, Oxford, that sounds great. It would be amazing to recover the cheese. I hope it hasn't ruined.'

'It'll be fine as long as they set the van to the right temperature,' Oxford assured him.

On the back seat, Albert coaxed Rex into getting up to make room for the extra man. Dave backed himself into the car and plopped down into the empty seat. Oxford waited for him to get his seatbelt on, then set off again, obeying all the highway code rules as he meandered through the town.

Rex sniffed the new man cautiously. He recognised him anyway – his cheese smell was literally unforgettable, but he took a moment to really draw it in and sort through it.

A right turn took them onto Fen Lane where Oxford drove past all the houses to a small industrial unit at the far end. Just past the last house, a gravel lane led around the back of the houses to two rows of four lockups. Each had a door and roller door, but no windows.

'We want number five,' said Donald, holding up the key with both hands to read the tiny label. Looking over his shoulder at the new man on the back seat, he stretched back to shake hands. 'Hi, I'm Donald. The cheese thief is my lodger.'

'Suspected cheese thief,' Oxford corrected. He felt it was important to keep his feet on the ground because his head was filling with images of getting his face on the front page of the Stilton Gazette. He could go from no one to local hero in the blink of an eye if he saved the festival. Dave's younger sister, Stephanie, would have to take notice of him then.

Buoyed by that thought, he parked the car and bounded from it. His companions were less dynamic, each taking their time to exit the car. Of course, one was overweight, one was nearly eighty and the other acted as if he were carrying around the weight of the world's problems.

Wondering if his luck might finally turn upward for a moment, Donald offered the young police officer the key. 'Here you go.'

Oxford backed away from it. 'I cannot touch that, sir. If I open the lockup, it is classed as illegal search. I'm on shaky ground being here to witness you opening it since I know you are not the person renting it.'

Albert snagged the dangling key from Donald's raised hand. 'Well done, PC Shaw. Don't jeopardise the prosecution's opportunity by doing something which you know you ought not to. I'll do it. I'm just a nosy old man in the right place at the wrong time.'

Rex was off the lead. Albert figured he could use the freedom to find a wall to water, which is exactly what he did. Then he sniffed the ground where a rat had widdled the previous evening. He generally found human behaviour bizarre and confusing, and today was proving to be no exception. He thought they were looking for some missing cheese; that was what his human said, but they were looking in the wrong place. They were opening the door over there, and the cheese was very clearly behind this door. He nudged the door with his nose to see if it would open, which it didn't. Curious now, Rex laid flat on his belly to sniff at the small gap under the door. Inside was a new vehicle, he could smell the rubber from its tyres, and the scent coming from one of those awful smelling air freshener things humans like to hang inside their cars. There was a myriad of other background smells to sift and sort but overwhelming all of them was the smell of Stilton cheese. It smelled just like the human they met at the hospital, who, inexplicably, was with them again now.

Two doors along, and oblivious to his dog, Albert faced lockup number five. The key slid effortlessly into the lock and turned as if the four-bolt mechanism were recently oiled. There was no handle to turn, just one to pull on so as the key removed the top, bottom, and middle barriers, it swung open with almost no effort on Albert's part.

With one foot over the threshold, he paused to look about for Rex. 'Come on, boy,' he called. The dog was lying in the dirt and staring under another lockup just along from Karl's one.

Rex looked up. His human was paying attention. Good. 'It's here!' he barked. 'You're looking for cheese, right? Come and smell over here.'

Unable to decipher the barking, Albert made his tone insistent. 'Come here, Rex. This is the one we want.' He could leave Rex to wander around outside but there was too much danger he would see a cat and run after it.'

Rex frowned. Maybe he had it wrong and they were playing a new game now. He bounced back onto his paws again but gave it one last go at explaining to his rather dumb human.

Oxford asked, 'Why's he got his paw up like that?'

Rex was sitting on his haunches like a good dog with his right front paw on the door to the lockup. Surely, they could understand that he'd found something.'

Dave laughed. 'I've seen dogs do this before. He can smell a rat inside or something. They can't control their natural instincts to chase rodents and such. I'll get him. You go on inside, Albert.'

Letting the security guard steer Rex toward the right lockup, Albert crossed into the dark space. Albert didn't know whether his nostrils would be assailed with a strong scent from the cheese if it were in there, or if it would be impossible to smell because it was inside a refrigerated truck. Either way, all he could smell was damp, dust, and old motor oil. However, when he stepped inside, looking around for a light switch, he could tell the cheese wasn't here.

Knowing he wasn't supposed to be involved until there was something to report, Oxford couldn't help himself from taking a peek. 'What've you found, Albert?' he asked hopefully.

Dave wanted to see too. 'Is it the cheese?' he asked as he went around Oxford to get inside. The lights came on as he crossed the threshold, Albert once again using his handkerchief to prevent leaving a fresh print on the switch.

As they blinked into life high up above their heads, several things became instantly clear. To start with, the lockup was filled with stolen goods. All around the outer edges and piled up along the walls were boxes of things no normal person would come to possess.

'Wow,' murmured Dave, as he bent down to inspect a pallet of DVD players – all the same brand, all in their boxes, and all quite certainly nicked at some point in the recent past.

Rex sniffed them too, curious enough to abandon the lockup with the cheese inside when the human who smelled of cheese said he should.

They didn't smell of anything interesting but that didn't mean he shouldn't mark them.

Albert saw his dog turn side-on to the stack of cardboard boxes and moved as fast as his old body would let him. 'Oh, no you don't, dog!'

Rex danced away as his human tried to swat at him. 'What? You mark them then if you want to. It's just some boring cardboard, you can have it.' With a scowl, Rex went back outside where there might be something he could mark without meeting disapproval.

Sighing with relief that the dog hadn't peed on the evidence, he then saw Dave reach out to pick up one of the DVDs.

Albert slapped his hand. 'Touch nothing,' he chided. Looking around as Donald came inside, he gave him the same advice. 'This lockup is filled with hooky gear.' Donald gave him a blank look. 'Stolen goods,' Albert explained.

'How can you tell it's stolen?' Dave wanted to know. 'Maybe the owner of this lockup is a fledgling entrepreneur trying to get a retail business started.'

Albert had a simple answer. 'Several decades as a detective gives a person a nose for such things.' He moved to the next pile which was alloy wheels for cars. They were still in their boxes and there were a lot of them.

Over his shoulder, he called to the police officer still waiting outside. 'PC Shaw.' Oxford poked his head through the door. 'PC Shaw, I am a concerned citizen called Donald Chessman. Twenty minutes ago, I called you to report that I chose to open the lockup of my lodger because I had begun to suspect the man to be involved in moving stolen goods. You, being a diligent police officer, were already suspicious that stolen goods were being trafficked in your area and had been compiling a short list of possible locations where they might be stored. When you received the call, alerting you to the likely presence of stolen goods, you rushed to this location to find Donald in this lockup, and believing the goods inside to be stolen, you called the appropriate division at your area headquarters in Peterborough.' Albert watched Oxford, waiting for him to react.

Oxford ran the statement through his head trying to make sense of it. Albert was claiming to be Donald and talking about a phone call Donald had made twenty minutes ago. He couldn't remember getting a call. He took his phone out to check it: nope, no calls from anyone.

'Call the station in Peterborough,' Albert begged, startling Oxford because the old man had snuck up on him and was now six inches from his nose. Albert was beginning to despair of the young officer. Back in his day, there were minimum intelligence levels for cops to demonstrate before joining up. He wondered if they had been lowered or just scrapped.

Stood at Oxford's shoulder, he dictated every word he wanted him to say and when the call was done and the radio silent once more, Albert clapped him on the shoulder. 'Well done, lad. This will be a feather in your cap.'

They were all outside the lockup, Albert shooing Donald and Dave back outside. 'Does this mean he will go to jail?' asked Donald who sounded ready to pass sentence and have the man shot.

Albert was going to answer, but he could see Oxford was about to speak and held his tongue.

'Yes, Mr Chessman, but only after he is found and arrested and then only once the goods are proven to be stolen and after a trial. However, given his record, and the evidence against him, it is likely the period between arrest and trial will be spent in jail.' That was clearly good enough for Donald who did a little dance of jubilation and looked something akin to pleased for the first time.

'I guess he escaped with the cheese though,' said Dave.

The large van-shaped empty space just inside the roller door hadn't escaped Albert's attention. He thought about the suitcases. 'Yes, that might be the case.'

'Either way, he's gone,' smiled Donald. 'I'm feeling like I should celebrate. I haven't had anything to celebrate in a long time. I'm going for fish 'n' chips. Who wants to join me? My treat.'

The mention of food made Albert's stomach rumble. The two cheese scones, which at the time had been heavy and filling, were now a distant memory. Good old English fish 'n' chips sounded wonderful.

Food got Dave's vote too.

Albert turned to Oxford. 'How long will it take a team to get here from Peterborough?'

He shrugged and curled his lip. 'I don't think anyone has ever been in a rush to get here before. Within the hour certainly. It's a twenty-minute drive but they won't have run out the door the moment I finished the call.'

It gave Albert and the others plenty of time to get to the chip shop, eat and return. As they set off, Rex leading because he knew the term fish 'n' chips when he heard it, Oxford called after them, 'Can you get me some chips?'

Mushy Peas

The village chip shop, aptly named Codswallop, was a five-minute walk from the lockup at the end of Fen Lane. Located in the High Street, Albert was surprised to find it busy at four o'clock on a Thursday.

'This is popular,' he commented as they approached, and it became clear they would have to queue.

Dave nodded wryly. 'It's only open twice a week. Thursdays and Saturdays. There just isn't enough call for it to be open more than that. No one wants it to close, so they get a lot of customers on those two days. The pub tried to serve fish and chips a few years back in direct competition with the chippy and the whole village boycotted them. They soon took fish off the menu.'

In the floor to ceiling glass front window of the shop, a sign boasted award-winning sausages. They were made to the chip shop's own recipe from locally bred Herefordshire Saddleback pigs and freshly battered to order. Albert's stomach growled deeply, and his mind was made up with no further deliberation required.

Pleasingly, despite the number of people wanting food, the queue moved briskly, and it was soon their turn to order. Albert insisted that he buy his own and would get for Oxford as well. The chips in his own meal would be split with Rex since the portions were always far more than a person could eat, but the battered sausage sounded so tempting, he ordered two and then a side of mushy peas which came in a small plastic carton with a lid. He handed over a crisp twenty-pound note and stood back with his order hanging from his left hand in a thin plastic bag while Donald and Dave placed their orders.

Dave looked quite content to have a perfect stranger buy his food though Albert could see on Donald's face that he regretted his spontaneous generosity as he selected a twenty-pound note from his own wallet. Dave added a can of lemonade to the order as the money exchanged hands and then stepped away as poor Donald had to root around in his pockets to find the extra change.

The lady working the till paused with the note halfway into the register. Donald noticed it, the change in his expression making Albert glance across at her. She bore a stern expression which hadn't changed at any point in the last ten minutes. Devoid of makeup, and with her hair scraped back and then stuffed into a net for hygiene, she peered over the top of her glasses at the money in her hands.

'Is something the matter?' Donald enquired.

'This is fake,' the woman announced. 'What are you trying to pull?'

Donald took a pace back as all eyes in the chip shop turned his way. 'I, I don't know what you mean,' he stammered.

Piercing him with her glare, she stepped away from the cash register and into the gap between it and the glass display of freshly fried food. Holding the note out, she said, 'It. Is. Fake. You've just tried to palm me off with a dodgy twenty-pound note. I'm calling the police.'

Albert stepped forward to pluck it from her hands. Her focus was all on Donald and she never saw him coming. 'Thank you,' he said, with a polite smile as he took it out of her reach and held it up to the window.

'Hey!' the chip shop woman screeched. 'You can't take that! It's vital evidence.'

Ignoring her protests, Albert wanted to know, 'Have you seen more of these?' It was fake, but it was a good one. He would never have noticed it for himself and had to hold one of the notes from his own wallet against it in order to see the difference. It was in the holographic image of the queen – the crown wasn't quite right. The paper felt the same, the images and placement was bang on. Whoever the forger was, they had done a good job with just one tiny error.

The woman didn't answer. Instead, she bustled to the end of the counter where there was a gap to get to the front of the shop: she was coming to get the fake note back. 'Martin, call the police,' she snapped to a boy behind the fish counter. 'We've caught a crime ring red handed.'

Albert hit her with his even stare. It was one he'd developed over many years of interviewing suspects and people he knew to be lying. In his experience, after a few hours of lying, suspects and witnesses always wanted to tell the truth. The lie just became too much effort to maintain and all it took was his knowing, silent stare to break down their walls. Using it on her now stopped her advance and changed her mind about snatching the note back.

'Yes, you should call the police,' Albert agreed. 'Young PC Oxford Shaw is currently at the bottom of Fen Lane. He won't be able to attend though, he already has a crime scene to guard, so you'll have to wait for a car to get here from Peterborough. You'll also have to close the shop to any further sales so the evidence can be preserved in it's current state.' Albert was making it all up as he went along, but the woman was buying it. A collective groan came from the people queuing to get their food.

'Ay? Close the shop? It's our busiest day,' the woman was thoroughly taken aback at the prospect of lost custom.

Albert allowed his face to soften. 'I'm a retired detective superintendent. I'm working with PC Shaw on a delicate matter which I cannot disclose but I can assure you this note will find its way into the right hands. Now, is this the first one of these you've seen?'

Behind her, Martin, unsure whether he was supposed to be calling the cops or not, decided he would stick with what he knew and started stirring the chips again. The teenage girl to his left took the next order and made a big thing of checking the note when the next person handed one over.

It wasn't the first time the chip shop owner, a lady called Pamela Harris, had been handed a dodgy note, but she didn't know how many she might have had. One turned up when she cashed in her takings to the bank a week ago and she'd been looking for them ever since.

Albert paid for Donald and Dave's order, handing over a good twenty-pound note to a grateful Mrs Harris as he placed the bad one in a separate part of his wallet. Getting fingerprints from it were so unlikely that he dismissed the notion but once they were outside again, he pressed Donald for an answer.

Where did the note come from?'

Donald was back to looking glum when he admitted, 'I found it on the floor in Karl's room last night.'

'In Karl's room?'

'Yeah.' Donald was looking down at the floor and scratching his right foot about in a distracted way. 'He didn't come home, and he owes me months of rent which he refuses to pay. I noticed the door was open and poked my head in. His room was the usual smelly tip it always is, but I noticed the corner of the note sticking out from under the closet door, and well, everyone recognises money when they see it, so I took it.' He chuckled. 'I guess this proves God has a sense of irony.'

Albert didn't know about that and had no intention of debating the subject. He wanted to get back to the lock up where Oxford would still be waiting for the officers from Peterborough to arrive. They would be there into the evening as they catalogued all the goods they found and attempted to cross reference them to goods reported as stolen. Hopefully, they would get a result and be able to nail Karl Tarkovsky, but the phoney twenty-pound note was vexing. Forging money was a whole different level of criminal activity. Modern notes were complex, multi-layered productions that required knowledge, equipment, and above all, money, to copy. It was not the work of a petty thief.

'I think I'll eat mine at home, fellas. I'm not feeling so good,' said Dave as he backed away. He already had his paper wrapping open and a handful of chips in his mouth. 'Thanks for this. Much obliged.' He didn't hang around to discuss it and had no intention of returning with them to the lockup on Fen Lane.

Donald frowned at Dave's back. 'Charming. You buy a fellow dinner and he doesn't even hang around to eat it with you. Some people have no social graces at all.'

Albert didn't disagree. But he did say, 'He had a tough night and has stiches in the back of his head. When I met him earlier, I thought he was concussed. He probably wants to have a lie down.' His explanation placated Donald, who'd already lost interest in the dairy's security guard.

With a quick tug on his lead, Albert got Rex heading in the right direction and his thoughts returned to the phoney twenty-pound note he now possessed. It would be easy to put it down to coincidence. Karl had come into possession of a dodgy note, maybe he didn't even know it, but he'd dropped it on the floor and Donald had found it. Nothing but coincidence.

Albert knew better than to believe in coincidence.

Loyalty and Honour

Albert puzzled over the missing cheese, the lockup full of stolen goods, and the dodgy money all the way back to PC Shaw.

The estimate for how long it would take cops from Peterborough to arrive proved to be inaccurate for they were already there and setting up. A police tape barrier was in place across the entrance to the small industrial unit but it surprised Albert to find it was Oxford himself who'd been positioned there to keep people away.

Handing over the paper wrapper full of chips, which Oxford then hid as best he could so none of the other cops would see it, Albert asked, 'How come you are here and not in there explaining what you found and how you found it?'

Oxford's annoyance showed through the moment he answered. 'The chief inspector kicked me out the moment he arrived. He said if he wanted to hear me speak, he would write down some lines first so I wouldn't sound like a complete idiot for once.'

All Albert could do was purse his lips. There was a stance one had to take sometimes with young cops so they remembered they were public servants and not Starsky or Hutch. Otherwise you found them rolling over the bonnet of their squad car rather than go around it. This wasn't it. Oxford probably had fantasies of catching Mr Big and getting a commendation but that was perfectly normal for a man his age. He didn't display such thoughts or dreams overtly and the chief inspector's behaviour defied explanation.

'Nevermind, lad. Eat your chips. Everything is better on a full stomach.'

Around a mouthful of his own chips, Donald wanted to know, 'What will happen next?'

'With the lockup and the stolen goods?' Albert sought to confirm, idly throwing a chip for Rex to catch now they were cooling down. Using his sausage to scoop some mushy peas, Albert savoured the fatty goodness the food delivered. It was sublime, and the sausages were worth the award they won with a hint of freshly cracked black pepper coming through at the end of each bite.

He savoured the taste for a moment before answering Donald's question. 'They will be here for hours going through it, I should think. Not the chief inspector, of course. This is below him. I'm surprised he even came. He'll make sure things are being done to his satisfaction and leave a sergeant in charge to sweep up. They'll put out a search for Karl Tarkovsky and his friends and will want to talk to you in some detail, I would imagine.'

Donald vacuumed up some more of his chips. He'd arrived at the bottom of his bag where they were soggy with grease and vinegar – the best ones, so far as Albert was concerned as he rooted around in his own bag to get to the bottom. 'I'm kind of stuck here then,' observed Donald. My car is back at the house and I can't afford a taxi.'

That he couldn't get home didn't matter, Albert thought. The police would arrange for him to be dropped back at his house once they were done with him but might request he come to Peterborough to record an official statement first.

Rex pawed his human's leg. It was getting close to dinner time and there was no sign of his dinner bowl. The chips were fine as a substitute but only if there were a lot more of them. He was getting thirsty too since his water bowl hadn't been seen in several hours.

'Sorry, Rex,' Albert put some more chips on the ground for the dog to devour. 'Oxford would you be a dear fellow and fetch a few things from the boot of your car? Rex here needs his dinner and some water I dare say. There's a bottle of water in the backpack for such emergencies so no need to go looking for any.'

Two minutes later, while Rex lapped gratefully at his water bowl and gave his thoroughly empty dinner bowl another lick – just in case – Albert broached the subject of the phoney money.

'Have you heard any recent reports of phoney twenty-pound notes coming into circulation?' The question was obviously aimed at Oxford, who needed a moment to clear his mouth.

'Counterfeit? No, why do you ask?'

Albert fished the dodgy note from his wallet and pointed to the error on it. 'Because Donald found one in Karl's room. It could just be coincidence.' Albert cringed that he had just said the word. It was his mantra that coincidence in policework never occurred. Recovering, he added, 'That's highly unlikely though.'

Oxford wiped his greasy fingers on a handkerchief from his pocket, then took the offered note. Just as he did, the chief inspector exited the lockup with one of the female officers from earlier hot on his tail still. He wasn't coming in their direction until he spotted Albert and Rex. Albert saw the man's eyes twitch in surprise and his direction change as he altered course. Albert took the note back and grabbed Oxford's bag of chips so they wouldn't be seen.

The chief inspector started speaking before he got to them. 'You are still keeping my officer company, I see.'

'You don't give this young man enough credit,' Albert replied, starting a whole new conversation at a tangent to the one the chief inspector was attempting to have. 'In the last few hours, he's interviewed a witness.'

'My witness,' the chief inspector interrupted.

Albert carried on as if the man hadn't spoken. 'Tracked a partial name to find a suspect. Tracked his address and gathered evidence that has led to the discovery of a lock up full of stolen goods. He did all that by himself, yet you have him standing guard at the perimeter. What is that? Punishment for using his brain?'

With a condescending smile, the chief inspector replied, 'Shaw stumbled across a name and got lucky. Nothing more. He'll get a pat on the back from the Chief Constable, but it will hardly change the national crime statistics. It appears to be a lot of low value, opportunistic thefts. The grand total of the goods in the lockup cannot be more than ten thousand pounds. I have the name of a suspect, and I'm sure we will pick him up shortly.'

'He's my lodger,' volunteered Donald. 'I'd like rid of him, please.'

The chief inspector looked at Donald for the first time. 'Thank you, Mr ...'

'Chessman,' Donald filled in the blank.

'Mr Chessman, good. Thank you. You have saved me a trip to come and find you. One of my officers will take a statement from you shortly and I'm afraid it will be necessary to search your home to look for more stolen goods.'

'I can take his statement,' Oxford volunteered.

Without a glance in his direction, the chief inspector repeated himself. 'One of my officers will take a statement from you shortly. One of my more competent ones,' he added snidely.

Fighting a losing battle to gain his superior's respect, Oxford chose that moment to announce the latest piece of information. 'A counterfeit twenty-pound note was found in the suspect's bedroom earlier today, sir.'

'Counterfeit?' The CI sounded genuinely interested for a moment, before realising that was how he sounded and making his tone disapproving again. 'Yes, well there are always counterfeit notes in circulation. Only the number and quality change. It's probably nothing more than coincidence. One thing you can rely on is coincidence to crop up in an investigation.'

Albert chuckled quietly to himself and stared at the floor so the senior police officer wouldn't see his smirk.

'Where is the note now?' The CI demanded.

With a hint of frustration, Albert took out his wallet again and handed over the dodgy twenty-pound note. He didn't need it as evidence, but he'd wanted to hold onto it for comparison if he came across another. 'Did you get any further with tracking down what might have happened to the cheese?' he asked as he handed it over. 'Karl Tarkovsky was identified as being the man at the dairy, you must know that by now. He rented this lockup and there is a van sized gap in the middle of it. In his house there were two indentations in the carpet where suitcases might have stood.'

'You were in his house?' the chief inspector asked.

Oops.

Oxford started to shrink as the chief inspector's eyes swung in his direction. 'Do you mean to tell me that you conducted an illegal search this afternoon. I'll have you fired, Shaw, and I won't have to do anything to achieve it. You'll do all the work for me.

'I let them in,' Donald interrupted.

'Ha! Yes, he did,' claimed Albert triumphantly, seizing the lie and holding on tight. 'PC Shaw was diligent enough to want to check out the address but was most forthright in stating that we could not go inside. That was until Mr Chessman here was kind enough to open the door and have us in for tea.'

The chief inspector looked from Albert to Donald and then to Oxford, slowly eyeing each in turn. Unhappy about being left out, Rex barked. The sudden sound made the chief inspector jump. 'Very well, gentlemen.' He handed the note to the female officer standing just behind him like an obedient pet. It went into an evidence bag and was gone. 'The investigation into Karl Tarkovsky is not for you to be concerned about.' He was looking directly at Albert when he made the statement but swivelled his head to make sure Oxford got the message too.

Oxford swallowed hard but didn't look away. He held the chief inspector's gaze until the senior man turned away dismissively and went to his car. The female officer raced around him to get his door, listened as he gave her some instructions, and then returned to take Donald to one side. She was going to take his statement and afterwards, drive him to his house where they would be met by another team.

The chief inspector was being efficient and swift, Albert observed. He might even be a decent copper, but his behaviour toward Oxford defied belief. When Donald went with the female officer, Albert asked about it. 'Why is the chief inspector so hard on you?'

PC Shaw half shrugged with one shoulder and mumbled something Albert couldn't hear. He was just about to ask him to speak up when Oxford chose to come clean. 'My dad was his boss when the chief inspector was a constable. Dad accused him of taking bribes, said he was far too friendly with some of his informants. There was a big investigation, but the chief inspector came out on top because they couldn't make anything stick, and that left my dad in a bad position.'

Albert understood what Oxford meant. Loyalty to one's fellow officer came above all other rules, except when honour was on the line. If the chief inspector had been proven guilty, Oxford's dad would have been given a pat on the back. When it went the other way, he must have been shunned by all the cops at the station.

'Dad quit shortly after that. Then he had a heart attack the following year and he never recovered. Even though he won, the chief inspector wants to get his own back on me. He's the one who arranged for me to be assigned to Stilton where, in his opinion, I can do the least damage to morale. Whenever he gets the chance, he gives me the jobs no one else wants, and goes out of his way to make me look bad. Because of him, most of the cops at the station in Peterborough think I'm a joke.'

Albert didn't like that. It made the man a bully. 'You know you can report him for unfair treatment. There are internal mechanisms for dealing with such issues.'

Oxford looked up from the floor with a wry smile. 'That would get me labelled as a snitch and a cry baby. It might get him off my back, but I would have to be able to prove bullying and that's never easy. It's more likely to make things worse because even if I do win, who would want to work with me afterwards? I'd be following in my father's footsteps, that's how everyone would see it.'

Albert had no argument to offer, and no words of advice that might prove helpful. Their chips were eaten, and poor Oxford was going to be stuck managing the cordon for the next few hours, so Albert, stifling a yawn, accepted that his adventure for the day was most likely over.

'I'm going to head to my lodgings, I think. Can you get my bags from your car, please?'

Oxford had forgotten about the bags. They'd been in his boot for hours now, since before lunch, in fact. Fetching them, he thought about how much they'd crammed into the day already. It was how he'd imagined his days would be when he dreamed about being a cop like his dad. His dad always told wild tales about chasing criminals and making arrests. He came home injured a few times when a suspect chose to fight instead of giving himself up. It was all minor stuff, of course. A bruise here or there, a black eye once. However, in Oxford's first year in uniform, he hadn't so much as made an arrest.

Handing over the backpack and suitcase, he asked, 'Where are you staying? I could get someone to give you a lift.'

It was good of him to offer, but Albert was happy to walk. The exercise would be good for both him and Rex, who most likely wanted to find a few trees to run around. 'No thanks, lad. Rex and I will go on foot. We're staying at The Crown, opposite the dairy, so it's not far to go.'

Nowhere was far to go in Stilton, it just wasn't big enough for two points to be more than a mile apart. Expecting that he wouldn't see the old man again, Oxford bade him goodnight and good luck. 'Thanks for your help today,' he called after Albert as he started to walk away. 'It was nice to feel like I was doing police work, and I learned some things. It was good ...' he started and stopped as he searched for the right words. 'It was good to have a mentor. I don't think anyone ever bothered trying to teach me anything before.'

Albert waved a hand. 'You're quite welcome, Oxford. I'm sorry we couldn't find a few more clues or have a bit more luck. It would have been nice to save the festival.'

'You really think the cheese is gone?'

The question made Albert stop walking. His instant answer was that yes, he believed Karl Tarkovsky had abandoned his thievery here and gone home. He would have stolen a refrigerated truck from somewhere and was probably halfway across Europe now on his way to Lithuania. He had two hundred thousand pounds worth of Stilton cheese in the back but most likely didn't have the brain to be able to shift it at a worthwhile price. But what if that wasn't the case? What about the forged money?

Because Oxford was still waiting for an answer, he said, 'Yes. I think it was taken straight out of the country.'

Then he walked away. Rex's lead in one hand, his small suitcase in the other, and a list of questions in his head.

Restless

The route back to the dairy took them past several green spaces where Albert could let Rex wander off the lead, but he waited until he found one with a handy bench to sit on. Albert had an apple in his backpack which he happily crunched while Rex followed his nose. The apple was a little warm from being in the boot of the car all day, but it refreshed his mouth after the greasiness of his dinner.

Comfortable and relaxed on the bench, Albert stayed there, with the sun setting behind the trees for fifteen minutes while he thought about Karl, the missing cheese, the money, and the life of petty crime that had gotten him nothing worth having. He turned to make a comment to Petunia and caught himself just as his mouth opened. His wife had been gone for a year already; long enough for him to get used to the idea, and it had been a long time since he absentmindedly tried to speak to her. Huffing out a breath that was a mixture of sad melancholy and anger at himself for feeling sad, he got to his feet and called Rex to heel.

At the pub, Albert had to go to the bar to find a person who could check him in. The man behind the bar turned out to be the landlord and owner, a man called Gerald Butler. He made a joke about not being the film star of almost the same name, a joke which went straight over Albert's head.

'Would you like a drink first?' Gerald asked. 'You must be tired from your day.' He was asserting a fact that might not be true in the hope that he could make a sale. Albert recognised the tactic, but he also accepted that he was thirsty. Pursing his lips as he perused the line up of drinks available, he selected a glass of stout and got a small one for Rex. Though he'd been on his feet a lot during the day and done a fair bit of walking, he elected to stand at the bar while he sipped his drink. He felt unexpectedly restless. The case had reached a dead end, the Stilton was gone, and his reason for visiting the village was up in smoke. That was part of the reason for his itchy feet, but more than that, he could not shift the feeling that he'd missed a vital clue already.

Rex's stout went into his water bowl which Albert fished from the backpack and the sound of happy lapping soon filled the air as the dog made short work of the drink.

Exhaling a hard breath of frustration through his nose, Albert delved into his pocket to get his phone. His finger hovered over the dial button as he argued with himself. 'It's the counterfeit money,' he told himself, speaking out loud though he hadn't intended for anyone to hear him.

'What's that?' asked Gerald, standing a few feet away as he poured pints of lager for a group of lads waiting for a football match to start on the big screen.

'Oh, nothing,' Albert replied hastily.

Gerald handed over the beverages and took the lads' money. Then he made a big show of checking its authenticity in the light above the bar. 'Can't be too careful,' he said when the young man who handed it over looked at him quizzically.

Cursing himself for speaking at an audible volume, Albert wasn't surprised when the landlord came over to talk to him. 'Get one in your wallet, did you?' he asked.

'What?' err, yes,' Albert replied quickly, grasping the suggested lie.

Gerald nodded as if he understood and had seen it all before. 'Yes, there's been talk between a few of the local shopkeepers. Dodgy twenty-pound notes have been turning up for the last week or more.'

'In the local area only?' Albert sought to confirm.

Gerald wasn't sure about that. 'I couldn't say where else they might be appearing, but they are cropping up around here.' It was too much coincidence for Albert to ignore. Taking his pint and retreating to a table when a new customer diverted Gerald's attention, he opened the contact on his phone and called his daughter.

'Hi, Dad.' His beautiful daughter, Selina, always sounded so bright and cheerful on the phone. 'Where are you now? Is it Bedford?'

'No, that's next, love. I'm in Stilton for the festival right now.'

'Oh, yes. Now I remember. That's where they chase the cheese through the street, isn't it?'

'Yes, love. Not this year though, I suspect. They've all been stolen.' He let that bit of news sink in for a moment as she repeated his words in a surprised tone. 'Yes, love, stolen. Actually, I wonder if you could do me a favour. I've stumbled across what I think is a money forging operation. I could do with ...'

'No, Dad,' she cut him off hard. 'You are supposed to be relaxing and enjoying the local cuisine. Chasing around trying to catch crooks at your age is just silly. You're retired, Dad. Do what retired men do and play golf.'

'I don't like golf,' he shot back, irritated that his daughter was telling him off. 'There's a local police officer here ...'

Selina cut him off again, 'Then let him investigate, Dad. It's not your job. And don't go calling Gary or Randall next to try to get them to find you information either. I'm sending them both a text message right now. Giving you information so you can dig into what's going on there just encourages you. Take it easy, Dad. Have a couple of gin and tonics. Get some sleep. Read a book. Do the things I fantasise about doing and enjoy the fact that you don't have to get up at three tomorrow morning and spend the day interviewing suspects.'

Now suitably irked, he used his dad voice. 'Now you listen here, young lady.'

'Young lady? Dad, I'm middle-aged. I'm not geriatric yet, though that hardly makes me young, but it does make you old. I love you, Dad. I just won't support you getting into trouble.'

'Ha!' he cackled defiantly. 'I can do a perfectly good job of getting into trouble without you to help or hinder me.' He wasn't going to get her to do a search for him; that much was clear, so before they got into a proper argument, he asked. 'How are my grandchildren?'

Selina sighed and let her father change the subject. 'They are fine, Dad. They miss you though. Apple-Blossom asked when you were coming home.'

For the next ten minutes, as Albert drank his pint of stout, they chatted back and forth about not much at all. Randall was supposed to be with him but had gone home with a concussion before Albert left Bakewell. Gary had agreed to take a few days off and was set to join him in York in six days' time. They were booked in for Yorkshire pudding lessons – another delicacy Albert had to buy in frozen bags now that he was a widower. Petunia made fantastic Yorkshire puddings all their married life. When the kids were young and still at home, Sunday dinners with a rib of beef were his undeniable favourite and she would make a tray of the towering, fluffy treats. Even when it was just the two of them once the children all left home, she still insisted on making them herself. "Those frozen ones are not the same," she would always say.

She was right too. But he couldn't make them for himself, and though he'd followed her hand-written instructions patiently several times, what for her would produce a mix that rose and crisped, for him became a soggy lump coated in oil.

Putting his empty pint glass down with a hard thump, he shook off the senseless and saddening bout of reminiscing and got to his feet. He already had the key to his room, he'd already eaten dinner, and there was nothing left for him to do. If the festival wasn't going to go ahead, there wasn't much point in hanging around in Stilton, but it was too late in the day now to go anywhere, so in the morning he would see what his options were between Stilton and Bedford and probably set off a day early.

Making his way to the stairs, an unwelcome thought resurfaced yet again – the forged note in Karl Tarkovsky's room wasn't there by coincidence.

Coincidence

H is room was spacious and comfortable. Far bigger than one might get in a modern, purpose-built, and characterless hotel, it boasted a large bathroom, a balcony overlooking the pub garden, and a fourposter bed complete with drapes. He wasn't expecting it, but the pub bore the name, The Crown, and it was a large building which might once have been something other than a waterhole for the locals. In his preparation for this trip around the country, Albert had read a few books for research, so he knew Stilton came alive as a stopping off place for weary horses. Several coaching inns sprang up to meet demand and it was due to the gathering of people that markets opened and the cheese trade developed.

Albert went through his usual routine of making up a space for Rex to sleep and making sure he had water in his bowl. Then he laid out his clothes for the next day and ran a bath.

Lying in the steaming water as he soaked his old bones, the feeling of restlessness wouldn't shift. There was something vital he'd missed today, but try as he might, he couldn't work out what it was. He wanted to claim it was something to do with the cheese and that he'd overlooked it because the forged note threw him a curveball. It remained elusive and frustrating.

At eight o'clock, it was dark outside but far too early to go to bed. After his bath he'd dressed in his cotton pyjamas, which needed a wash, he observed, but were good for one more night. Rex watched him from a corner of the room he'd claimed as his own. Albert had a book to read. He'd even taken it out and left it on the bedside table, but it held no interest and he worried he just wasn't going to get to sleep with the mystery going around and around in his head. He opened it in a bid to obey his lovely daughter's wishes, and a piece of paper dropped out where he'd placed it as a bookmark.

Picking it up, he chuckled to himself. It was the betting slip from the turf accountant in Melton Mowbray. He ought to have thrown it away, but something made him keep it – just in case it was a winner. He didn't even know how to check or how long the ticket remained valid, but it served as a fun reminder of the caper he had there and the fabulous pork pie he made with his own two hands. Reminiscing, however, reminded him how good he'd felt when he solved that particular mystery.

With a growl at himself, he kicked off his slippers. 'Do you fancy a walk, Rex?'

Rex bounced off the carpet and onto all four paws in a single move. Evenings were a boring time when there was little chance of getting anything to eat and no chance of anything exciting happening. A walk changed all that. There were critters around at night who slept during the day and he didn't often get to chase.

When his human started putting his outdoor clothes on, Rex spun on the spot in excitement. They were going for a walk and they were in a new place, yet another new place, in fact, since they seemed to arrive somewhere different every few days at the moment. He was fine with it. Each new destination yielded a new set of smells and new trees for him to leave his scent on.

It would be hours before the pub shut its doors, so Albert had no concern about getting locked out when he left. He didn't exactly have a destination in mind, he just wanted to be out of the room so he could see things and revisit places in the village which might jog his memory.

Opposite the pub, the dairy sat dark and quiet. He remembered Mrs Graves and her *delightful* teenage daughter. Had she and the Board been able to come up with a way to save the day? To save the festival? He'd forgotten they were working on a plan to get hold of enough Stilton to carry them through the weekend, remembering it only at that moment. Maybe the festival would go ahead after all, but in an abridged manner. That would be something at least.

Standing at the low wall that bordered the dairy, Albert could see the buildings, but didn't know which was which. In the morning, he was due to have his tour. It was still booked, but unlikely to go ahead. Matilda might not have been much help, but she had been quite clear on that one point. He could check in the morning and get his money back if the tour would not happen.

A cool breeze blew from the east, ruffling Rex's fur as he too stared into the dark of the dairy. It still stank like cheese so far as he was concerned. It might all have been stolen but that had done little to diminish the smell. Was it important that it was back where they stopped to eat the chips? His human and the new human who'd been driving them around today seemed to want to find out where it had got to but didn't listen to him when he found it. Maybe he misunderstood what the humans were getting excited about. It wouldn't be the first time: humans are just so strange.

The same cool breeze chilled Albert's head, making him fold his collar up and, not for the first time, wish he still had hair. Packing to set off more than a week ago, he laid out all the things he thought he might need for a long road trip tour of the country. He needed to pack light because he had to carry whatever he took, but even so, he should have remembered the need for a hat.

Staring at the dark buildings, he wriggled his lips back and forth, urging his brain to make a connection. When none came, he gave Rex's lead a light tug and moved on. Turning away from the village centre, he walked away from civilisation but took a right before he reached the edge of the houses. Stilton being such a tiny place, it didn't take him long to navigate back to a place he recognised and found himself at the entrance to Fen Lane.

Wondering if Oxford might still be stuck down at the lockups, he decided to check. It wasn't far to go and he was curious to see if they had found anything more exciting than the low value stolen electronic and other goods that were easily visible.

Rex's ears pricked up as he caught a scent of someone coming the other way. The breeze carried the scent of cheese mixed with a musky men's deodorant and sweat so he knew Dave was approaching long before his human bumped into him.

At the edge of the village, as they approached the lockups tucked away there behind the houses, the streetlights did little to illuminate the countryside. A canopy of trees and no ambient light from a nearby city meant the landscape was properly dark. On a moonlit night he might be able to see fine, but away from the houses, Albert felt like he was walking through ink soup. Too busy watching where his feet were going, he got quite a shock when Dave appeared around the corner.

They startled each other, both making a surprised noise and sucking in a swift lungful of air as they automatically danced back in fright.

'Goodness,' said Albert, clutching his heart. 'It almost stopped that time. Whew, you came out of nowhere.'

Dave sagged against the wall, gasping for breath, and Rex looked from one human to the other and then back at the first and sighed with despair. For such capable creatures, they were really rubbish at using their most important sense.

'Are you heading back to check on Oxford?' Dave asked once he'd levered himself upright.

Albert said, 'Sort of. Rex needed a walk, but I was curious to see if they had found anything interesting among the stolen goods.'

'He's already gone for the night,' Dave let him know. 'I had the same thought. After I ate my chips, I had a little nap and felt a lot better. I think I was acting a bit weird this afternoon. I'm starting to think I might have a mild concussion.'

Albert felt certain the doctors at the hospital would have ruled that out before they discharged him but had to agree the man had been acting strangely. Choosing to avoid making a comment, he asked, 'Are they finished there already?'

Dave shook his head and glanced back at the lockups. Having almost collided with Dave as they both reached the corner at the same time, the lockups were still shielded from Albert's view but he walked around now so he could see too. The police were still down there, a pair of spotlights on tripods erected to cast some light and the hum of a small petrol generator chugging away to power them. A couple of teenage boys were sitting astride their bikes, leaning on the handlebars to watch proceedings, though they decided they were bored and cycled away just as Albert looked.

Dave said, 'They told me Oxford was relieved an hour ago. You used to be a cop, right? How long will it take them to empty the lockup and leave? I mean, it just looked like a load of junk in there, but they don't look like they will finish any time soon.'

Albert chuckled. 'Things have changed a lot since I was on the force. Heck, they don't even call it the force anymore. It's the service now because the force sounds too aggressive or something.' Albert rolled his eyes, remembering his eldest son telling him about the proposed change in name. He thought it sounded like nonsense then and hadn't changed his mind yet. 'To answer your question though, I think it will depend on how many other crimes they are able to sew up with this discovery. All the different piles of goods in there might each represent a separate reported theft. They could clear a list of crimes and, if they are finding fingerprints or other physical evidence, they might be able to catch multiple criminals. They'll be trying to find Karl Tarkovsky, but I doubt he's in the country. I reckon he took the van full of Stilton and fled, getting across the channel before anyone even had a chance to report the van stolen, let alone the cheese.'

'I'm sure you're right,' Dave agreed. 'It's a shame for the festival. And for the dairy, but they'll recover sure enough. The insurance will pay for it and it's not like suppliers can go elsewhere to get it. Stilton isn't Stilton if it's made by anyone else,' the security guard said knowingly. He lapsed into silence and neither man spoke for a moment. It became an awkward silence after about ten seconds, at which point Dave said, 'Well, must be off. Goodnight.'

'Goodnight,' Albert called after the man as he vanished into the dark again. It was good of him to check on Oxford, especially given the day he'd had.

Albert watched the police working in the lockup for a few seconds as he continued to chew over the misalignment of clues in his head. The counterfeit note didn't fit. In fact, the only way he could make it fit, was to assume it appeared in Karl's room out of pure coincidence, and he didn't like that at all.

Unable to shift the feeling that he was blind to the truth, he turned around and started back towards the pub. Perhaps a gin and tonic to help him sleep was in order. The imagined taste hastened his steps, but he might have walked faster yet had he known what waited for him in the bar.

Murder Victim

By the time he got back to the Crown public house, his lodging for the night, he'd been out for almost an hour so he felt that by the time he'd had a drink and warmed up, it would be an appropriate time to be getting to sleep. The concept of a small something for supper appealed too – a packet of crisps or some salty peanuts perhaps.

He got neither, for the moment he appeared in the bar, a young man came barrelling toward him. Rex saw him too, the human moving faster than one might expect which sent him into protection mode until he smelled who it was.

'Albert,' called Oxford who was all but running to get to him. 'I figured you were out walking Rex when you weren't in your room.'

Albert was surprised to see the young police officer again so soon. 'Good evening, Oxford. I expected that you would have gone home when they finally released you from the crime scene down at the lockups.'

'I nearly did,' Oxford admitted. 'But I decided to check back at the cottage first. What the chief inspector said earlier about there always being forged notes about. I remember one of the criminal law professors lectured about it when I was in training. Anyway, I thought I would spend a few minutes to see if there were reports of counterfeit notes in the area. Usually we would get a bulletin advising us to report such things if there is a known batch, it prevents lots of different people all looking into the same thing.' He remembered who he was talking to. 'Of course, you know all this already.'

'What did you find?' Albert prompted to get to the point. 'Have there been lots of incidents recently?'

'Sort of. It's quite recent and very localised. That's not why I came here though. I need you to come to the cottage. Can you do that?'

'Right now?' Albert wanted his gin and tonic and the packet of peanuts he'd decided on.

Oxford pulled a face which said right now was what the situation required but he didn't want to say that because Albert was old and might need to get to bed. Albert deciphered PC Shaw's expression, checked the time on his watch, and figured he could get to the cottage and get back before last orders.

'Come on, lad. Let's go. You lead, I'll follow. Maybe you can tell me what this is about on the way there.'

Oxford had stripped out of his uniform but still had his squad car outside. Albert didn't think the young man was supposed to drive it in his jeans and hoody; it made him look like he'd stolen it, but he kept quiet about the matter so he could hear what Oxford had to say.

Oxford didn't say anything. Except to say that it would make more sense to show him.

At the cottage, all it took was a flick of the mouse to bring the computer screen back to life. By the time Oxford had manoeuvred around to get another chair and positioned Albert in front of the monitor, Albert was already looking at some rather horrible pictures.

'Is that just one person, or parts of several?' he asked. On the screen were pictures taken at the scene of a murder. There was no chance it was an industrial accident: it looked like a slaughter.

Oxford pulled up his chair next to Albert's and leaned over to press a button on the keyboard. The pictures advanced each time he pressed it. 'It's two men; the murder victims the chief inspector spoke about this morning. They were killed sometime in the night, maybe eighteen hours ago now. I tried to find the coroner's report, but it hasn't been attached to the file yet.'

'How did you even find this?' Albert wanted to know.

With a half shrug, Oxford said, 'It's in a central database. Anyone with a password can access it. If you mean to ask how I knew to look at it, then the answer is blind accident. I clicked on the wrong file.'

Coincidence. The word popped into Albert's head mockingly.

Pushing the thought from his mind, he turned to look at Oxford. 'I have to assume you are showing me this for a reason. How does this link to the missing cheese or Karl Tarkovsky?'

Oxford puffed out his cheeks. He'd been utterly certain until right this moment, but he'd dragged the old man here now, so he had to at least admit why. 'I think one of the victims is Karl Tarkovsky.'

Albert's head snapped around to look at the screen again. He'd seen worse in his life; he knew how gruesome murder scenes could be, but he hadn't seen the like in a long while and it was turning his stomach. He didn't bother to ask if the killers had removed parts to make the bodies harder to identify; they must have, or the police would have worked out who it was while still at the scene. Tilting his head, and tapping the same key he'd seen Oxford use, he advanced a few frames.

'Why?' It was simple enough question. 'What is it about those bodies that makes you think one of them is Karl? You can't recognise his face because he hasn't got one.'

'Tattoos.'

Albert looked again, leaning closer to the screen, and putting his reading glasses on so he could make out fine detail. 'Well, you've got me there, kid. I can see ink, but I cannot tell what is what and what I can see is mostly covered in blood.'

'May I?' Oxford was asking if Albert would lean back so he could lean in and take control of the keyboard and mouse.

Albert shuffled slightly, letting the young man do what he needed to, but as Oxford brought up the mugshot of Karl Tarkovsky, Albert was already working through what this could mean. He didn't get to explore his thoughts because Oxford wanted to draw his attention to a tattoo on Karl's neck.

'I remembered this from when I first saw it. I remember wondering what it was because it looked like the tip of a wing, like if he had big angel wings tattooed right across his back.' Oxford stood to demonstrate the size he meant and pointed it out on the screen with the tip of a pencil. 'See that bit right there?' He showed Albert Karl's mugshot and the portion of the inking that curled over his trapezius muscle. Then he clicked back to the crime scene shots on a different tab and pointed again. 'That's the same bit of ink right here.'

Albert squinted at the screen and sucked on his teeth. He didn't want to tell the boy he had it wrong. He couldn't be certain that he did. Truth be told, he might even be right, but it was tenuous at best.

'What do you think?' asked the young police officer, his tone betraying how unsure he also felt.

Satisfied that staring at it any longer wouldn't change his mind, Albert settled back in the chair. 'It could be him,' he acknowledged.

Oxford was out of his chair and doing a victory dance instantly. He got up so fast, he startled Rex who leapt to his feet and barked his displeasure. 'Hey, human. I was asleep, thank you.'

Albert waited patiently for the young officer to calm down and kept his tone kindly. 'I said it could be him, Oxford. We don't know that it is. All you have is a possible partial match on a tattoo.'

'Yeah, but I could tell the chief inspector. They have the body so would be able to do a full match of his tattoos. Or they can do a DNA test from his remains. That's an easy yes or no question if you are trying to match it to a single person. If I'm right, they'll be able to work out who the other body is I bet.'

The kid was desperate for some recognition. He wanted to solve actual crimes and chase real bad guys, not hang around in a peaceful village and bug old ladies about double parking near the church on a Sunday morning. He might be right about the body, but was telling the chief inspector the right way to go?

'What if you are wrong?' Albert sowed a seed of doubt which killed the smile on Oxford's face. 'What if you give the chief inspector a bum steer?' He could see Oxford begin to panic at the thought of such a scenario. Before he could say anything, Albert helped him out. 'We should make sure. Find out a little bit more and then go to the chief inspector with something solid, don't you think?'

'I guess,' Oxford said, sounding reluctant to do anything now. 'I definitely don't want to give him bad information.'

'No. Of course you don't. We can work this out though. Let's suppose it is him. What does that tell us?'

Oxford had one instant answer. 'That Mr Chessman doesn't have to worry about his lodger coming back.'

'Yes, I suppose I cannot fault you for the accuracy of that answer, but I was thinking of something more pertinent to the particular problem you and I have spent the day pursuing: the cheese might still be here somewhere.'

The light of truth shone down on Oxford's skull, illuminating his brain, and filling his mind with images of the people of Stilton erecting a statue in his honour for returning the cheese and saving the day. Would he look good in a cape, he wondered, as the possibilities sought to overwhelm him.

'Hello,' said Albert, popping the bubble of glory that Oxford found himself temporarily trapped inside. Seeing the kid's eyes focus again, he asked, 'Did you go somewhere nice?'

Oxford looked embarrassed when he mumbled, 'Erm, ah, what do you mean?'

'I was talking to you for the last two minutes and you weren't taking any of it in. You were off with the fairies somewhere. Now that you are back, I'll try again. Yes, the cheese might still be here. If that is Karl Tarkovsky, and I'm not convinced it is,' he added quickly, 'then it trashes my idea that he took the truck and his suitcases and went directly to the nearest port. It doesn't make it any easier to find though. Was he killed by the buyer? Was he ambushed by someone else? Petty criminals tend to make enemies, and friends, out of people who are unsavoury to say the least. I think we should assume that whoever killed Mr Tarkovsky and his friend also took the truck full of Stilton. Solve his murder and maybe you solve the question of where the cheese is, but maybe you don't. Maybe they didn't take the cheese? Maybe it will take years to catch the killer or killers. What do you say to that?' Albert put Oxford on the spot, testing him to see how he might respond.

'We won't know unless we try?' asked Oxford tentatively in case it was a trick question.

Albert slapped him on the arm. 'That's the spirit.' The sudden noise in the quiet room made Rex jump again. Awake once more and beginning to get irked at the humans' constant need to disturb his sleep, he eyed them both and thought of ways to get his own back later.

When his dog stopped making grumpy noises and settled again, this time with his back to them, Albert let his own mind wander. Solving this case was going to take a leap of faith. They didn't have a lot of clues to follow, but if he went with the premise that one of the freshly murdered men in the pictures was indeed Karl Tarkovsky, then it gave them a direction to explore.

'Where was he killed?' Albert asked, staring at the screen again in the hope the information might leap from it.

Oxford had access to that and more. 'The bodies were discovered by a gang of highways agency guys at the edge of the road near Yaxley.'

'Where's Yaxley?'

'On the way to Peterborough. Almost halfway there, in fact. The bodies were dumped just to the side of the road in some bushes. There was no real attempt to hide them; no shallow grave.'

Albert took a moment to consider that. Dumping the bodies was brazen, and in his experience only those who held no fear over getting caught would be so bold. That indicated a different level of criminal, one who saw crime as a business and the police as an inconvenience to bribe, blackmail, or threaten. As a small ball of worry formed at his core, he let the young PC know his thoughts. 'Oxford, I think I should tell you that this may be the work of an organised crime gang.'

'Gangsters? Here in Cambridgeshire? I don't think so,' Oxford smirked, thinking the idea ridiculous. 'Farmers, yes. We have lots of those. What would make an organised crime mob come to the countryside?'

It was a good question, even if it did come via a flippant response. Why would they come here when all the action is in the city? And what would they want with a truck full of cheese? A yawn split his face. 'I need to get some rest, kid. The murderers and cheese thieves are sleeping peacefully in their beds right now. We ought to be too. In the morning, we can look at this with fresh eyes.' He pushed off his chair, using the desk to lever himself upright.

Oxford stayed in his seat. 'What about the festival? We have so little time to find the cheese. Shouldn't we be putting in all the effort we can until we've exhausted every opportunity to get it back?'

Albert gave the young man a kindly pat on his shoulder. 'If you have the energy and will to do that, lad, you should make yourself a strong coffee and crack on. I'm going to let myself have a nightcap and get to bed. The years add up, young man. The years add up.'

Breakfast

The nightcap never happened, and Albert slept without the numbing aid it promised. Oxford drove him back to the pub, but by then, the yawning was almost uncontrollable and dictated Albert get straight to bed. There was no argument from Rex, not that he expected one, but pulling the covers up under his chin, Albert's tired brain continued to spiral as it tried to connect the missing Stilton, the counterfeit money, the lockup full of stolen things, and a double murder.

The pub had a restaurant on the side which also catered breakfast for the guests staying upstairs. There were five rooms, each filled with guests in Stilton for the festival, Albert assumed. Coming into breakfast with Rex at his side, four couples lifted their eyes to see the newcomer. They were all middle-aged or older; man and wife pairings whose kids had grown up and left home already.

He nodded and murmured a brief hello as the landlord, Gerald, appeared through a door on his right with two heaping plates of breakfast. The rising steam carried the heady scent of freshly grilled salty bacon and peppery sausages. It made Albert's stomach do a little flip of excitement and remind him that supper had never happened.

Rex looked up at his human sniffing the air. 'You can smell that, can you? Hoorah, the human's nose works! I could smell that upstairs in the room while I was still asleep.' If he knew how to shake his head despairingly, he would have done so, but his human was paying no attention, and Rex had just spotted a piece of bacon on the carpet. It was beneath a table and between the feet of a lady having her breakfast, but that didn't mean he wouldn't be able to swiftly snag it on his way past.

He lined up on his prize as they wove between the tables.

'Good morning,' Gerald greeted man and dog once he'd delivered the breakfast plates to a hungry couple by the window. 'Sit anywhere, please. I'll be over to take your order shortly.'

Rex squinted at the bacon. His human was talking to another human, creating a delay that was undoubtedly unnecessary. 'We are talking bacon here folks,' Rex harrumphed to get his human moving again. They started forward again. This was it. He just needed a few more feet and the bacon would be his. His lead stopped moving, jerking his head unexpectedly when he reached the end of the slack. Spinning about to see what might have caused the latest delay, Rex found his human settling into a chair. 'What are you doing?' Rex asked, his whine of disappointment getting his human's attention.

Albert looked down at Rex. His dog was puffing his cheeks out with each breath as if upset about something he couldn't articulate, and glancing across the room. 'What is it, boy?' Albert leaned down to see if there might be another dog with one of the couples.

'It's right there,' whined Rex. 'Look at it. Doesn't it look delicious? I can even see some fluff on it where it has been kicked across the carpet. Oh, my goodness, you have to let me go over there to get it.' Rex lifted one paw and placed it meaningfully on his human's thigh for good measure as he looked up to make eye contact. 'I know humans are fairly dumb, but please try to understand the message I am giving you.'

'Is it a squirrel?' Albert asked. 'Did you see a squirrel outside of the window?' Rex hung his head in sorrow. 'There's a good boy. After breakfast, we'll go for a nice long walk and see if we can't find a piece of parkland for you to run around. There's bound to be squirrels you can chase there.'

With a resigned grump, Rex dumped himself on the carpet and stared at the piece of bacon, wondering if he could convince it to come to him. Feet arriving by his face turned out to belong to Gerald, the landlord.

'Everything is cooked to order so there will be a slight delay. Can I get you started with a pot of tea or coffee and some toast? The bread is made fresh on the premises every morning. It's our own honey whole wheat recipe,' he boasted proudly.

Whatever it was, Albert thought it smelled delicious, and across the room he could see it was served cut into thick slices with lashings of butter. He ordered the full English with black pudding, bacon, sausages, fried eggs, beans, mushrooms, grilled tomato, and more tea, then tucked into the two slices of toast Gerald brought out with his first pot.

Beneath the table, Rex licked his lips. The bacon smell was driving him a little bit nuts. He'd been for a walk and eaten his breakfast already; his human was good like that, always dealing with Rex's needs first. But not being hungry meant nothing whatsoever when it came to bacon. He could see the layer of glistening white fat running around the edge and he needed it.

Not for the first time, he considered chewing through his lead. The relative distance between his teeth and the bacon had to be about the same distance as his lead. His human had looped it under one foot of his chair, as was his practice but there was room for Rex to get under the table and across the floor to it. He judged the gap between the table leg and his human's leg and went for it, barging through the gap with mindless determination when he discovered he was, in fact, wider than he thought.

At table height, his human was protesting and questioning what Rex might be up to, but Rex was nearly there now and he wasn't stopping for anything. He just needed to go under a chair, across the gap between the tables and snag the delectable treat from under the lady's feet.

He didn't really fit under the chair though, so obstacle number one proved to be quite a challenge. His shoulders stuck so the chair ended up riding him as he tried to shimmy across the carpet on his belly. By rolling onto his side a little, he shook off the chair, but his human was hissing at him now and demanding he come back. He would have to hurry because the next move his human might employ could be to grab his lead and haul him back.

So close! Rex was already salivating. The salty goodness would barely register, he would eat it so swiftly, but his focus was too singular now to consider abandoning his quest.

Then the feet appeared again. On the far side of the target table, Gerald was collecting plates. 'How was your breakfast?' he asked the couple, receiving compliments in return which he promised to pass along to the chef, his wife, by the way. The couple got up and left and that made the task all the easier.

Rex was nearly there. He wanted to grab the bacon without the lady noticing but he would dive on to it if he had to. Behind him, his human's hissing took on a new level of urgency, but this was it. He leaned forward to daintily pluck his prize from the carpet and a hand picked it up in the very moment before he claimed it.

It was the landlord again!

Flabbergasted to have been robbed at the final hurdle, Rex bounced to his feet. In so doing, he hit his head on the lady's now empty chair to knock it over, which tripped Gerald as he made his way back to the kitchen with the empty plates.

Food spilled as the plates crashed to the ground and a cornucopia of treats bounced on the carpet like manna raining from heaven. It was all three feet farther away than Rex could hope to make his lead stretch, but unable to resist, he lunged anyway, throwing his bodyweight forward in a bid to snag something tasty.

Behind him, his human made a noise that sounded like, 'Ulp!' and the lead came free in a whoosh.

Gerald had a piece of unwanted bacon rind hanging from his right ear. He was trying to right himself, while at the same time ignoring the pain in his right shin where it collided with the chair, and also attempting to work out why the chair had attacked him. However, when he swung his head back to look at it, what he saw was a large beast coming at his face.

He screamed, much like a little girl, his wife would later assure him, as the dog rushed forward and licked his ear.

The piece of bacon rind got swallowed so fast Rex's taste buds had no chance to register it, but he was already vacuuming up a piece of cold toast, some mushrooms, a grilled tomato and the famed piece of bacon that drew him into this quest in the first place.

Oh, joyous day! Rex wagged his tail and licked a broken plate covered in congealed egg yolk.

A swat on his rump caught Rex's attention and spun him around to face the danger. Only, when he looked, what he found was his human looking down at him with an expression somewhere between incredulous disbelief and anger. He also looked wet, which a sniff revealed to be tea.

Rex sat and wagged his tail. 'What happened to you, my human?'

Stallholder Riot

I t was more than thirty minutes later when they left the pub for the day. Albert returned to their room to change his trousers since the tea made it look like he'd experienced a 'senior moment' and wet himself. Rex got left in the room while Albert gave breakfast a second attempt and apologised, not for the first or last time, to Gerald for the mess.

Oxford hadn't been in contact or left a message, which defied Albert's expectations. Not that he knew the lad, but he felt he had a handle on the young man's spirit so half expected him to be waiting in the pub at breakfast this morning. He didn't have Oxford's number; an oversight on his part when he should have thought to take it, but the walk to the cottage wasn't a long one. It was already mid-morning, giving him less than two hours before his supposed tour of the Stilton dairy, not that he expected it to go ahead, but he intended to go there on time to find out since he was unlikely to ever come this way again.

With Rex leading the way – the dog ought to be filled with chagrin but if anything looked pleased with himself – he left the pub behind.

The sun was out and blue skies dominated which gave the country village an alluring feel of welcome, and the air, which yesterday had been cool and tinged with moisture as it threatened rain which never came, was now charged with the delights of autumn. Somehow, as if the villagers had saved their best days for the festival, everything about Stilton looked brighter and better today.

The pair did not get far before they began to see stall holders setting up. This wouldn't be the main event, which wasn't until tomorrow – a full day of activities starting with the race through the village with the cheese – this was people getting in early to get set up and maybe snag some early sales from the tourists flooding to the area.

They paid him no attention as he wove his way past them. They were too busy bolting together the scaffold poles that made the frames of their stores and arguing with each other about how close they were to the other stall selling cakes. Yet another group were adding flowers in baskets to hooks on the lampposts and stringing final lines of bunting. When they turned onto the High Street, there was a pair of men on stepladders reaching up to erect a large sign welcoming one and all to the Annual Stilton Festival. Directing their actions was none other than Mrs Graves.

Seeing her, Albert gave Rex's lead a quick tug to change his course and made a beeline for her. 'Good morning,' he hallooed.

She had a clipboard in one hand and a pair of running shoes on her feet which clashed with her otherwise polished office-wear look. The shoes were white with a pink swoosh down the sides whereas her thick leggings were black, as was her calf length skirt. They were topped by a long camel coloured winter coat which looked to have cost a few quid, but it sort of impressed Albert that the lady chose comfort for her feet over fashion for the task which most likely involved a fair bit of walking.

She didn't take her eyes off the banner when Albert spoke. 'No, Tom. To your left and up a bit.' She held up a finger to beg a moment's grace from Albert. 'We have to get it even. Mark, stop moving your bit for a second.'

'This is heavy, Cecelia,' Mark pointed out.

'Good thing you're a big strong man then,' she shot back, unconcerned about his aching muscles.

Albert waited patiently for a few more seconds until Mrs Graves was content that the banner was correctly positioned and turned her attention his way. The men, both in their mid-twenties, tied the banner off now that she was happy and shook their arms to relieve the ache setting in. 'Hello,' she replied, her eyes betraying that she didn't recognise him.

'We met at the dairy yesterday briefly. You were just running into an emergency meeting about the cheese,' Albert reminded her.

'What about the cheese?' asked Tom, who was now down from his ladder and carrying it over his right shoulder. 'What emergency?'

Her cheeks coloured fast and she blustered, 'It's nothing for you to be concerned about, Tom. The matter was resolved.'

'What's going on?' asked Mark, joining them though he'd left his own stepladder where it was against the lamppost.

Tom frowned and shook his head. 'Dunno, Tom, she won't tell me. Some kind of emergency with the cheese.'

'I told you, it's nothing,' she replied, this time more coolly and with some force. 'It was a matter for dairy management, not something one of our truck drivers needs to know about. Anyway, the matter was resolved.' Finished talking to the two men, she took Albert's elbow to guide him away, back toward the mouth of the High Street where there were no people to overhear them.

'Have you been able to locate a replacement supply of cheese?' Albert enquired, mystified as to how they could come up with enough cheese to save the festival in less than twenty-four hours.

'No,' hissed Mrs Graves. 'No one knows, okay? We must keep it that way. If the villagers find out the Stilton has been stolen, there'll be panic in the streets.'

Albert suspected that was a gross exaggeration but didn't comment. Instead, because he felt he had exposed a secret and felt a little embarrassed by his faux pas, he asked about the tour. 'Are the tours going ahead today? I wasn't able to get a definitive answer yesterday.'

Mrs Graves sighed as she let her shoulders slump in defeat. 'No. All the tours are off until production has replenished at least some of the stock. The tour involves showing visitors the various stages of the cheese production. We can still show them the fresh cheeses being made because fresh ingredients arrive every day, but then we lead them through the maturing sheds so they can get a feel for just how much cheese we produce and ship. The rows and rows of Stilton have always produced awe-inspired gasps and we do cheese tasting with the tour groups. That gives us a chance to try different flavours out on them and has led to some successful derivations of the main product.'

'Like Stilton with cranberries?' Albert guessed.

'Exactly right. Look, I'm sorry the tour has been cancelled. If you can come by the visitor centre later this afternoon and ask specifically for me, I'll refund your money and give you a coupon to return for free with some friends if you can make it back here another time. I'm afraid I still have a lot to do setting up today. If you'll excuse me?'

Albert had one last question. 'What are you going to do if you cannot get hold of enough cheese and the stolen Stilton isn't recovered? Surely, the festival won't go ahead and all this setting up is pointless.'

Again, she sighed. 'The rest of the Board and Mr Brenner are still working on that. We've reached out to our main customers, but while they all pledge their support, very few of them keep much stock. They buy it and ship it and a lot of what we manufacture goes directly out of the country. We might be able to replace about two percent of what we lost. Before you ask, no that isn't enough to cater the festival. Not by a long shot.'

The sound of approaching footsteps brought their attention around to the High Street where they saw several men and a woman bearing down on them. They were led by Tom, who had his phone in his hand and an angry look on his face. Moving fast enough that he had to slow before stopping, the angry-looking Tom, switched to speaker setting and held his phone in the air at mouth level. 'Say that again, Auntie Edith,' then to everyone one else, he said, 'Listen to this!'

'I said, "It's all gone, love. All the cheese has been stolen. There's not a drop left unless you count yesterday's batch." We're not supposed to be telling anyone. That Mr Brenner swore all the staff in the hâloir to secrecy – those of us that knew anyway. I could lose my job just for admitting the truth, can you believe that?' Auntie Edith had spilled the beans when prompted, the enraged Tom undoubtedly choosing to call her when he became suspicious.

Mrs Graves was teetering on the brink of out and out panic. The group of people already facing her with their angry expressions, were being joined by more and the villagers came to see what might be occurring.

'There's no cheese!' shouted Tom, turning to face up the High Street. His shouts were heard by everyone within fifty yards and swiftly passed along to those who were out of earshot. In seconds, a rabble was forming. With the secret out, Tom turned back to Mrs Graves, a woman who he didn't like simply because she was in charge.

When he raised a finger to prod her in the chest, Albert decided it was time to change the course of the conversation. 'Rex, guard!' he said loud enough for those nearest to hear.

Rex had been watching the situation develop with interest though he wasn't sure what it was all about. The humans were getting excited about something, but when his human gave him a command to deal with the man with the angry face, he needed no further encouragement. Able to shift from passive to bloodthirsty in a fraction of a second, he drove off with his back legs to leap at the aggressor. There was a finger poking out and he was going to try to bite it clean off.

His lead jerked just before he got to it, correcting his forward momentum so that his teeth snapped at fresh air. The effect was much akin to firing a gun in the air as the front row of the rabble all took a collective step backward from the insanely barking dog.

Albert knew Rex would leap, leaning his own bodyweight in the other direction so Rex would frighten, but not injure, when he lunged. The dog yanked at Albert's shoulder joints, wrenching them painfully, but the effect was exactly as Albert hoped and the rabble quickly backed away.

Grasping the opportunity suddenly presented, Mrs Graves raised her hands to beg for calm. 'Yes, the cheese has all been stolen. It happened on Wednesday night and Dave Thornwell was injured in what must have been a violent encounter with the robbers. The dairy is working on the problem of making sure we have enough cheese to support this weekend. The police are looking for the cheese and it may yet be found so I must ask you all to be calm and give us time to find the solution we all need.'

Albert reeled Rex back in even as Tom and his cohort surged forward once more. The dog kept them back a sensible distance, but the shock of his attack hadn't done much to dampen their ire.

Rallying the support of the crowd, which was still attracting yet more people to it, Tom came at Mrs Graves again. 'Give you time? What time? The festival is tomorrow! Where are you going to find hundreds of Stiltons by tomorrow?'

'We are doing all we can,' Mrs Graves countered weakly.

'By hiding the truth from us?' Tom raged at her and got a lot of support from the crowd now facing the lady from dairy management. 'Forget the impact of lost revenue when the visitors get here tomorrow and there's no cheese. The visitors will busy themselves with what they can do and eat the food that the stallholders have available, but do you think they will book to come back next year?' He was shouting now. 'Do you think we will ever recover from this? What will you tell the crowds tomorrow when they come to Stilton and find we haven't got any? What about the race through the village chasing the cheese? Shall we make some papier-mâché ones and hope no one spots the difference?'

Albert could see Mrs Graves flinching from the onslaught. None of this was her fault and though she might be here enforcing the policy of secrecy, it most likely wasn't her policy. Either way, yesterday when they discovered the missing cheeses, it was already far too late for anyone to do anything about it: the crowds were coming and maybe the dairy management genuinely believed they would be able to do something drastic to avert disaster.

As Tom readied his next barrage, Albert stepped into his personal space. 'I think that's enough now, young man.'

'Who are you?' Tom growled.

'Just a man out walking his rather large former police dog.' Rex chose that moment to lick his lips, an action, that while not deliberate, was certainly well timed. 'Mrs Graves didn't steal the cheese, and I can testify that the police are working all hours attempting to fix this issue. Do you think it decent and gentlemanly to be wagging your finger at her the way you have been?' Albert jutted his head forward and turned it so his ear was aimed at Tom's mouth. When no response came immediately, he probed further. 'I see you feel confused about your role here. This is what the police refer to as inciting a riot. It carries a maximum sentence of three years. If property damage or injury to persons then occurs, the sentence can escalate sharply.'

Tom suddenly looked less sure of himself and some of the hecklers at the back were choosing to wander off, deciding now that their stalls might need their attention.

Narrowing his eyes, Albert dropped his voice to almost a whisper and stared squarely at the mob's leader. 'You were very rude and aggressive toward Mrs Graves. I believe you owe the lady an apology.'

With folded arms, Albert waited for it. Until Tom opened his mouth that is, when he seized the moment and spoke loudly, 'What was that?' I didn't hear you.'

'I'm sorry,' Tom mumbled.

Albert could have insisted he say it louder, but instead, now that more people were drifting away and Tom looked suitably sheepish, he leaned forward from the waist again, and spoke quietly so only those nearest him would hear, 'Go away.'

If Tom had anything further to say, the words went with him. It left Albert and Rex alone at the mouth of the High Street with an astonished-faced Mrs Graves.

'Who are you?' she asked.

'Special Agent Smith, MI6. The old man outfit is just a disguise. I'm actually thirty-six beneath this rubber facemask.' Albert responded without taking so much as a heartbeat to think. When her jaw dropped, he burst out laughing. 'I'm just an old man who used to be a police officer many years ago. I've met a lot of men ... people, I should say, like Tom. They are easy enough to deal with if one knows how.'

'Well, thank you for stepping in. I've never seen the people here like that. It was scary.'

Albert wriggled his lips in thought and huffed out a breath. 'It probably isn't over, I'm afraid. They'll go into a huddle when the dust settles, and when they get to talking, some bright spark will suggest they should all go to the dairy to demand answers. It won't occur to them that anything that can be done is already being done. Crowds possess an intellect level equivalent to the square root of the number of people contained therein. They will distract from the effort of others to justify to themselves that they are the valiant ones trying to force their leaders to act.'

Mrs Graves looked utterly terrified by what Albert was telling her. 'You think they might yet riot?'

He had to give the question some thought. 'No. No, I don't think so. It's a quiet village where everyone knows everyone. They won't start turning over cars and setting fires, but they might march on the dairy and make trouble there.'

She was tearing at her handbag, yanking it open to root around inside. 'I've got to call Mr Brenner. He'll need to know what might happen.'

Albert doubted that would make any difference, but he stood back and let her make the call.

Many miles away, a conversation about the cheese was taking place.

Thieves

'Your instructions were simple, were they not? You were due to arrive this morning and yet I find that you are not parked outside my bunker as arranged. Now you tell me that the product I paid a handsome advance for is still in Stilton.' His voice was calm, but the man listening to it wasn't fooled into thinking he was going to be reasonable.

'I experienced some unexpected complications,' the thief attempted to explain.

'No. You made your plan too convoluted,' the calm man countered. 'All you had to do was steal the cheese and deliver it to me. It should have been easy for you, and you were being well paid. You also told me you could do it.'

'Yes. But delivering the cheese only to get caught for the crime would have led back to you. I needed to make sure my tracks were completely covered for both our sakes. The plan will still work, I just need a little more time.'

'You are a bungling incompetent fool and now you threaten to reveal me as the buyer if you get caught.'

'No, no!' the thief quickly argued. 'That is not what I meant.'

'Good. Because I shall happily have you killed if the police ever look my way. You know I have the money to arrange it.'

Not for the first time, the thief questioned his own sanity. The buyer approached him directly many months ago. He wanted the cheese, not that he said what it was for, but he wanted it all and he was prepared to pay for it – more than market value too, which seemed ridiculous. Who was he to argue though? A quarter of a million pounds, fifty thousand up front which he was to use to obtain the truck without stealing one which, the buyer assured him, would get him caught the moment he passed a motorway smart camera. The sum was too tempting to ignore. He would never make that kind of money by himself. If he saved every penny for the rest of his life, he'd never scrape that much together.

So he agreed to steal the Stilton. All of it, and the buyer was painstakingly specific about when the crime had to take place. He was informed well enough to know there would be almost fifty percent more cheese right before the festival so that was when it had to happen.

'I will get it to you in the next couple of days. I just haven't been able to retrieve it yet.'

'Tell me what it is that is preventing you from setting off right this minute,' demanded the calm man at the other end.

'The police mostly. They don't know anything,' he added quickly, thinking he'd made it sound like they were onto him. 'They are just physically in my way. Plus, Stilton is a tiny, close-knit village and I can't risk moving it during daylight. Someone would see the truck with me at the wheel and I would get caught. I will go for it tonight and you will have your cheese tomorrow morning. I just have to wait for it to get dark and the village to go to sleep.'

'The truck with my cheese is still in the village!' His cool demeanour finally burst. 'Are you stupid, man?'

'It was the only way the plan would work,' the thief explained, taking the role of the calm one for a moment. 'I haven't been able to get to the truck due to an unforeseeable turn of events. A coincidence no one could have predicted.'

'You are being vague,' accused the calm man, irritation creeping into his voice. 'You also said mostly,' he quoted the thief. 'If it is mostly the police, what other obstacles do you have to overcome?'

A flash of annoyance made the thief's lip curl when he said, 'There's this old man and his dog.'

Sleepy Head

Albert watched the villagers and stallholders warily as he made his way along the High Street between them. He wanted to take a longer route around to avoid their stares but would never allow himself to employ such a cowardly tactic. Instead, he held his nerve and kept his head high as he took the direct route back to the cottage. The faces watching him were hostile, and when he passed Tom, he could see the young man murmuring something to a gaggle of other men as they all tracked his path.

He knew it wouldn't take much to convince the young men to do something stupid.

They didn't follow him though. If Tom felt like having a word with the man who put him back in his place, it was going to come later: Rex represented too great a threat to consider mounting an attack now.

The cottage looked sleepy and quiet; no sign of life coming from within as Albert made his way down the garden path. He followed it around the side again to the door beneath the antique blue police light. Looking up at it again, it took him back to an era when police call boxes still existed and could be found dotted all over the country. He had to wonder what had happened to them all. No doubt most were gone by the time Dr Who made them famous, though he knew there was one still in place outside of Earl's Court tube station.

He knocked on the door and stepped back while he waited for an answer. No answer came until he was about ready to try the handle for himself. Then a sound of someone moving about reached his ears and a shadow falling across the beam of light inside the door preceded it opening. Oxford had the look of a person who had just woken up.

Because he had.

With a yawn, which he tried to cover with the back of his right hand while simultaneously stretching and twisting, he managed to say, 'Sorry. I stayed up all night going through the case file and all the old files on the system for Karl Tarkovsky.' The yawn refused to be suppressed and split his face in two as it overtook his desire to speak. Once he'd wrestled his fatigue back under control, he continued, 'Then I looked at his known accomplices and anything else I could find that might shed some light on what he was doing and why he stole the Stilton.'

Impressed by his dedication, but at the same time thinking the man probably should have gone to bed sooner since the morning was almost over and he'd slept through it, Albert stepped over the threshold. A sniff of the air inside the small police office convinced him of two things. 'We should open a couple of windows,' he said as he let Rex's lead go and headed toward the nearest one. 'And you should head home for a shower and a shave.'

'No, I'm okay. I can keep going,' insisted Oxford as another yawn threatened to flip the top of his head off.

Giving him a level stare, Albert said, 'Kid, you stink.' The statement made Oxford sniff himself and realise the funk a full twenty-four hours had managed to create. 'You'll need a clean uniform too. I think there might be trouble today. You may yet find Stilton to be the place you make your first arrest.'

Taken aback, Oxford blustered, 'Hey, I never said I hadn't made my first arrest.' He hadn't, and all the cops in Peterborough knew it, but the old man had no way of knowing that.

Albert raised his hands in surrender. Making your first arrest is a lot like losing your virginity for a police officer. The longer it takes you, the greater the pressure from your peers and the more deeply you begin to doubt yourself. He could tell Oxford hadn't taken that step yet; through no fault of his own, of course, but he let the young man lie about it without challenging him.

'Go. It'll take me a while to go through your notes anyway. You did make notes, right?'

Oxford nodded as he crossed the room and sat back at the computer desk. A shower sounded good. As did some breakfast, though it would be more like brunch by the time he got it. He survived the night on coffee and biscuits, but there were fewer biscuits in the pack than he remembered, and the packet had suspiciously moved position. Nevertheless, Albert was right about his need to get clean and find a fresh uniform.

'It's all here,' Oxford pointed to a thick A4 pad on which many handwritten notes were added, 'and here.' He showed Albert the many open tabs on the computer. 'Hopefully, it will all make sense. What I found was ...'

Albert held up a hand to stop him. 'It will be best if I read it unbiased. That way, when you return, we can compare opinions and see if they meet anywhere.'

Yawning again, Oxford nodded his assent, grabbed his hoody from the back of the computer chair and staggered, drunk with sleepiness, from the cottage.

Standing at the desk, Albert flipped the A4 pad and read a couple of the notes. It was time to crack the case, he felt. With a glance down at Rex, he said, 'There's something missing from this equation, boy. Do you know what it is?'

Rex tilted his head. His human was asking him something; he could tell by the inflection in his words.

'Tea,' announced Albert. 'Tea is missing.' There was water in the kettle, which he discarded first. 'One should never make tea with previously boiled water,' he explained to Rex. 'The process of boiling deionises the water which reduces its ability to infuse with the rich tea flavours.'

His human wasn't saying anything worth listening to and he could smell the empty biscuit packet in the wastepaper bin. There being nothing else going on, he turned around twice and flopped to the carpet.

Albert made tea with just a splash of milk and settled in to start reading the notes. There were thirteen open tabs on the computer, an infernal contraption which he saw little need for. He had a rudimentary understanding of how to use it though and could move the mouse to the tab bit at the bottom of the screen to open the different pages. Over the next half an hour, he pieced together a rough pattern for Karl Tarkovsky.

Karl was a career criminal, but Albert knew that already. He was the kind of thief who was always dreaming of the one big job that was going to change his life. Get the inside track on one big job and retire to Rio de Janeiro like one of the Great Train Robbers. What criminals like Karl ignored, was that the Great Train Robbers all got caught. Every last one of them, despite the conspiracy theorists who romanticised the crime and made out that there were others who managed to get away. Just like them, Karl always got caught, but this time, if Albert stuck with the theory that Karl was one of the bodies on tab number one, then he'd pulled his last job and it had gone spectacularly wrong.

His murder suggested that he was either working with someone who double crossed him or working for someone who always intended to dispose of the loose ends.

Halfway down the first page of Oxford's notes, he'd circled a line about a parking ticket, then drawn a line and written three dates. That intrigued Albert. He clicked through the tabs until he found a page relating to it.

Two weeks ago, Karl had parked in Flint Lane in Peterborough – the address, postcode and time of the offense were noted on the ticket. He'd duly paid the ticket, but Oxford's next line of notes read "There's nothing there." Albert wasn't sure what that meant, but when he scrolled down on the ticket page, he saw two more parking tickets for the same address. Each time, he had stayed longer than the maximum permitted time and been fined for doing so. Each time he had paid but then went back and did it again. It was inexplicable behaviour for a man with no job - parking fines were not cheap.

It wasn't much, but it was a corner to pick at.

Back at the first tab, he cross referenced the pictures of the second body against those of Karl's known associates. Each of his 'friends' was a scumbag just the same as he with a record as long as a person's arm. However, like the children's board game, Guess Who? Albert was soon able to eliminate most of them due to one or more physical attributes. It would have been easier if the bodies had heads, but he made do with what he had, and once again found a tattoo that matched. This time, the match was less tenuous, a word written down a forearm. It wasn't in English, but he didn't need to understand it to know it was the same one. Moreover, if the second chap was one of Karl's associates, then the first body had to be Karl. Just like that, they had two dead Lithuanian scumbags. Karl Tarkovsky and Filip Fiske.

Albert chewed the inside of his cheek and stared at the ceiling for a moment while he thought about what this might mean. For starters, the obvious conclusion was that the cheese was gone. The buyer decided not to pay and killed the two men who stole it. Wait a second though; Dave said there was a whole gang. Certainly more than two because he said he saw or heard three different men, one of which he identified as Karl. So was there a third body? Or was the third person the killer?

That sort of made sense because, as Oxford pointed out, there wasn't enough profit from the cheese to make it worthwhile once it was split between a gang. However, if the mastermind killed his crew and sold it to a buyer keeping all the profit for himself ...

Albert went back to the list of known accomplices and to Oxford's notes. Two of the five men listed were in jail so they could be eliminated. Another one was dead, Filip Fiske's body found alongside Karl's. That left just two: Darius Balthis and Jokubas Kaleckas. Either one or both could be guilty. In his head, Albert was making a list of things he wanted to check out. It started with contacting or going to where the second dead man, Filip Fiske, lived. Had he packed a suitcase as well? Had he said anything to the people he lived with? Finding out what the man had planned might tell them a great deal, or it might tell them nothing. Or he might live alone.

Before he could consult the notes any further, Oxford came back through the door to startle both Albert and Rex. The trace of stubble on his young face was gone, replaced by fresh, dark tanned skin as his schoolgirl's complexion shone through. His neatly pressed uniform pleased Albert like an inspecting officer on parade, but he set all that aside to ask a question.

'Did you identify the second murder victim?'

Caught halfway through the door, Oxford had an answer, nevertheless. 'I think it's Filip Fiske, although I'm not sure I'm saying his name right. I spotted a tattoo on his forearm in the mugshot that matches the one on the victim. Sorry,' he added. 'I would have got here quicker, but I went back to check they were all done down at the lockup, but they were only just packing up. Sergeant Boswell estimates that there was nearly a million quid's worth of stolen gear in the lockup. I bet Karl didn't even know how much he had, and he'd have been selling it for almost nothing I bet.'

Albert's eyebrows reached for the top of his head. 'They worked all night.' He hadn't expected it to take that long and it showed a level of diligence he hadn't expected. 'I have to wonder how it is connected to his death, but the bit I still cannot connect is the counterfeit note.'

Oxford shrugged. He hadn't given it any thought. 'Maybe it's just coincidence like the chief inspector said.'

Albert doubted that, but he let it go for now. 'All right, Constable Shaw, what do you think our next move should be?'

Oxford took a moment to think. He liked that the old man was giving him a hand. Left by himself, he would most likely have done as the chief inspector ordered and given up on the case a day ago. Albert was giving freely of his time and sharing his wealth of experience while asking nothing in return. Now he was on the spot, and though the old man would give him a steer, this was a test to see if he could think things through for himself. They had options to explore.

Without answering, Oxford stalked around Albert to get to the A4 notepad. 'I want to do several things at once. Since that isn't possible, I guess what I must do, is find a sensible order and tick them off as swiftly as I can. I've been trying to work out what happened between stealing the cheese and the double murder. I need to speak with Dave again because he wasn't certain about the number of men in the gang, but they took his shoes and whacked him on the head. I think he knows more than he realises. I might do that first, but then I want to go Filip's house. He was a lodger just like Karl except he lived with a couple just outside Peterborough.'

'What about the parking tickets?' Albert prompted. The boy was doing well so far; thinking logically and questioning what he was being shown. 'On your notes, you wrote that there is nothing at the location where he got the tickets. I assume that was what you meant anyway.'

'Yes.' Oxford went to the computer, sliding into the seat and opening a fresh search engine. Moments later he had an aerial view of the area on the screen. 'It's right about here,' he jabbed a finger. 'It's a load of restaurants and bars and bookkeepers' places. Or rather it used to be. The buildings are still there but the area died out as a place to go years back. They haven't changed the parking restrictions though, so people leave their cars there and get fined because the traffic wardens know they can get an easy mark there and they are expected to meet certain numbers each week. Parking was originally limited because the businesses needed to load and unload, that's why he got fined for staying there too long, but if you look at the times when he was fined,' Oxford clicked to the tab with the parking fines on it, 'you see on each occasion the tickets were given at just after ten o'clock. The parking zone enforcement comes into effect at nine o'clock so he must have been there all night.'

Albert slapped Oxford on the shoulder. He hadn't spotted that himself, not that he felt bad about it given the cursory examination he had time for. 'Well done, lad. I think you're onto something there.'

'How can you tell?'

'Gut feeling. It feels wrong. He's there all night and leaves so late on three occasions that he gets a fine. Maybe he leaves that late more often but doesn't get caught the other times. What is he doing that keeps him there all night? If it were a residential area, I would assume he had a girlfriend, but that's not the case. It's something else.'

'What is it then?'

'We don't know that yet. However, I think you have done some solid work here. We should find Dave and reclarify what he saw and heard.' A thought occurred to Albert. 'Can you transfer those mug shots to your phone? He might recognise one of the other men.'

'I can do better than that, I have a laptop, but he said he didn't see their faces,' Oxford reminded the old man.

'True. But people often don't realise what they saw. Showing him a face might jog his memory. He got bonked on the head, after all. We can quiz him and then check out where Filip Fiske lived. That will put us close to Peterborough and we can have a look at the mysterious Flint Lane.' With a whistle to get Rex up and on his feet, Albert was ready to go. The excitement of the hunt, that was what kept him working too many hours when he was serving. He hadn't realised how much he missed it until recently.

Dave

They found Dave at his house in Varnes Road. Or, to be more accurate, they found him returning to his house on Varnes Road. Oxford and Albert spotted him at the same time, as the dairy's security guard made his way back along the road toward his house.

A convenient parking space outside the house next door allowed Oxford to swing his squad car in and be on the pavement to greet Dave. 'Morning, Dave.'

'I haven't been anywhere,' he said defensively.

Albert raised an eyebrow.

'Okay,' said Oxford. 'I want to show you some mug shots, Dave. Have you got a few minutes now?'

Dave's feet were twitching on the spot. He wanted to get to his house it seemed, but Albert, Rex and PC Shaw were blocking his route. 'I'm really busy actually, can we do it another time?'

Albert's other eyebrow raised. 'Busy doing what?' he wanted to know. 'You're the night security guard and it's daylight, plus all the cheese has been stolen so you should be falling over yourself to help this young man recover it. One might be given to think you don't care about the cheese and the festival.'

Dave sagged under the old man's words. 'Yes, yes, of course, sorry. I'm just getting some chores done, that's all. They can wait, obviously.' He indicated toward his house. 'Please, come in.'

Inside Dave's house, a small terraced house in a village filled with small terraced houses, the décor was aged but tidy. Walking through the house, it was clear to Albert that the man lived alone.

At the kitchen counter, in a long galley kitchen which led to a bathroom at the back of the house where once the outhouses were exactly that, Oxford set his laptop and poked it into life.

'You know I didn't see their faces, right?' Dave reminded both men.

Albert felt his lips twitch as an answer formed but he kept his mouth closed so Oxford could lead – it was his investigation, not Albert's, he reminded himself.

Oxford had the mugshots ready but took a moment to explain an important point. 'That's right, Dave, you did tell us that. I need to inform you that the investigation has grown beyond a simple case of robbery. It is now a murder investigation.'

'What!' Dave couldn't hide his surprise.

'The name you gave us: Karl Somethingski, turned out to be Karl Tarkovsky, a known thief with a long criminal record. You know that part already, but what you don't know is that immediately after stealing the Stilton with his associates, he and one other man, who we believe to be,' he clicked the mousepad to open the tab with Filip's file, 'Filip Fiske, were brutally murdered.' Dave looked ready to vomit. 'Their bodies were found at the side of the road just outside Peterborough at about the same time you were being rescued from the chiller. Our working theory is that either the buyer, or a third member of the crew, killed Karl and Filip once he had no further use for them.' He turned the laptop, so it faced Dave. 'I have two pictures for you to look at. Take your time, please. You may have seen something but didn't realise it.'

Dave shook his head at the futility of Oxford's request: he hadn't seen their faces, but he leaned on the counter to scrutinise, first Filip's face and then Karl's, since Oxford showed it to him for good measure, and to jog his memory if that was possible. He stared at the pictures for several seconds but then gave them the answer he knew he would before he looked. 'I'm sorry, guys. I never saw them. They were inside the hâloir and I was outside. They must have spotted me though, because one of them clobbered me on the head and stole my shoes. Then they threw me in the chiller like I told you.'

Undeterred, Oxford clicked the mousepad again. 'How about this man?' On the screen was the mugshot for Darius Balthis. Oxford remained silent, watching Dave's face to see if he registered any recognition. 'He is another known associate of both Karl and Filip. He could be the mastermind behind it, or he could be their killer.' When

Dave continued to stare, Oxford clicked the mousepad once more to show him Jokubas Kaleckas.

Albert was also watching Dave's face, his eyes in particular because they always betray the truth when the mouth four inches south might be lying. Dave wasn't lying though; he'd never set eyes on any of these men.

Trying to give them something and not just say no to every question, Dave volunteered, 'I think I would recognise their voices if I heard them again.'

With a resigned sigh, Oxford closed the laptop. 'Thank you for looking, Dave. If you think of anything that might help, even if you think it to be insignificant, please contact me. I'm not giving up yet.'

'Of course.' Dave nodded his head vigorously. 'Likewise, if you can think of anything I can do to help, just let me know. You know where I will be.'

It was a throw away sentence, a fake offer because he didn't expect they would call on him, but it gave Albert an idea. 'Actually, Oxford,' Albert got in quickly while his mind continued to think things through. 'I think I would benefit from seeing the crime scene.'

Oxford and Dave both said, 'What?' but for very separate reasons.

'I thought we were going to Filip Fiske's place next?' queried Oxford.

Albert nodded to himself as a picture began to form in his head. The picture was based on a wild idea, a real leftfield, out-of-the-box concept that couldn't be true, but might just make everything else make sense.

Remembering the need to speak, he said, 'We were, Oxford. First, as a quick detour, I would really like Dave to show me the chiller and the hâloir where the criminals, Karl and friends, loaded the truck.'

'Isn't that all in the crime scene team's report?' Oxford felt there was little to gain from revisiting the hâloir. He'd already seen it and there really wasn't much to see. It was nothing but an empty space now.

Albert started backing toward the front door. 'The crime scene report isn't complete yet though, is it? We don't have a full list of their findings.'

It was true, Oxford acknowledged, following Albert to the door. The old man hadn't steered him wrong yet; he could indulge him a look around the dairy. Over his shoulder he called, 'Are you coming, Dave?'

Blood at the Dairy

D ave jumped into the front of the squad car for the short ride and had Oxford park at the main office next to reception so he could stick his head inside and let someone know why there was a police car on the premises. He said it would prevent someone from management coming over to question what they were doing.

Rex didn't like the dairy. The smell from the cheese was simply too strong for his powerful nose to handle. Admittedly, the stench had diminished since yesterday but only by a small amount. The absence of all the mature Stiltons for more than twenty-four hours had allowed some of the smell to dissipate, but Rex believed it would be years before the scent would truly leave the place – it had seeped into the walls. Yesterday morning when they arrived, he'd been able to detect a trace of blood in the air. Not fresh blood, but recent, like from a deep but not life-threatening wound. A day ago, it was almost intangible, just a vague scent on the air. Today, as they approached a building that must have contained the cheese – it stunk so badly – the smell was somehow stronger. It told Rex he was homing in on where the blood was, but the overwhelming smell from the cheese, even though it was absent, was making anything hard to pinpoint.

'This is the hâloir,' explained Dave as they approached a thick-sided old brick building with two large modern doors on the front. 'Cheese would be aged in caves if there were any around here. That's certainly how it was done in much of the country when they began to produce Stilton here, but in the 18th century, when they built the dairy, they built this place. The walls are thick, and the temperature remains a steady five degrees centigrade all year round. In the height of summer, it can get up to seven degrees inside, but that's still cool enough for the cheese. They added these doors ten years ago for better humidity control.'

Using a panel on the side, Dave flicked a switch and the doors began to open.

Surprised by the security guard's depth of knowledge, he put it to one side so he could ask, 'Where was the truck?'

Using both arms to show width, Dave walked in front of the doors. 'Right here. It was backed up like our trucks would do. That's why I couldn't see them. The truck's back end is between the doors leaving about a man's width either side.'

Albert walked over to roughly where the front of the truck would be. 'Then you were about here when the fella came from behind and hit you?'

'Yeah, I guess so,' said Dave. 'Caught me completely by surprise. I remember the blow, but I don't remember anything after that.'

Albert looked down at Rex. The dog was sitting idly on his haunches, sniffing the air in a bored kind of way.

'Do you want to see inside the hâloir?' Dave asked.

Oxford waited for Albert to answer. He really didn't know that they were doing here. There was a double murder to investigate, and if they were going to find the cheese, they could be certain it wasn't here.

Albert had been staring into the distance as he let his brain make random connections but clicked his tongue to get Rex moving again. 'Where's the chiller?' he asked abruptly.

The chiller was in the building next door, which also housed Dave's little security shack. One of the other security guards was in there doing not very much when Dave opened the door.

'Hi, George,' said Dave as he startled the man inside. George had his feet on the desk and a tablet in his hands on which he was watching a soccer match. The bank of security monitors was being ignored, not that there was anything worth watching on them, but Albert wondered how many firms employed security because it reduced their insurance payments, but ended up with a lazy bloke in a booth watching TV.

George almost fell over in his haste to get to his feet and stash the tablet in case one of the dairy's bosses was outside. 'I was, ah, I was just checking the scores for a minute,' he babbled.

Dave waved a hand to stop him. 'It's okay. It's just me.'

George put a hand on his chest. 'Whoo! You scared me. No one ever comes down here. I thought maybe it was management.'

'No chance, mate,' chuckled Dave. 'I'm not sure they even know where the security office is. I'm just showing Oxford the chiller.'

George peered around Dave to see outside his little room. 'Sure, yeah, whatever, man.'

'Well, I thought I'd better let you know because we'll appear on the monitors in a minute.'

Now it was George's turn to chuckle. 'Yeah, like I ever look at those.' Both men laughed, their jobs were a big joke to them.

'Tell me about it,' said Dave, shaking his head because it was that funny. When the laughter subsided, he led Oxford, Albert, and Rex to the chiller.

Rex's nose was twitching now. Albert bent down to speak quietly to him. 'What can you smell, boy?'

'Blood,' Rex replied without needing to think. 'Behind those doors is human blood.' He knew his human didn't understand what he was telling him, so he was going to have to try to make him see once they were inside. Just to be sure, he gave the air another sniff. 'It's his blood,' he pointed his nose and eyes at Dave.

Albert straightened himself, watching with curiosity as Dave pulled the floor and ceiling bolts, then grabbed the handle to open the door. 'As you can see,' said Dave, tapping the floor bolt with his foot, 'once they threw the bolts, there was nothing I could do to get out.'

It certainly proved his innocence, unless one considered that he might be the inside man. He'd been acting odd since Albert met him. At the start, Albert assumed it was just a mild concussion making his actions seem out of place, but more and more, he began to wonder if Karl and friends locked him in on purpose. Why then would he name Karl? Ok, he'd only given them a partial name, but it took Oxford less than five minutes to find Karl Tarkovsky. If Dave were involved, naming his accomplices was the dumbest thing he could do. Not the inside man then ... Keeping quiet as his brain continued to filter ideas and scenarios, Albert followed the others into the chiller.

Rex needed about eight seconds to find the source of the blood. It ought to have been on the floor where the unconscious form of Dave the security guard lay and bled, but it wasn't. It was above Rex's head. On the corner of a stainless-steel shelf, there was blood, skin, and a few strands of Dave's hair. Rex could detect the same shampoo the human used. He had to get up on his back legs to sniff it, using one front paw on the shelf below to support his weight.

Albert saw his dog find something and moved in.

Dave saw it too and laughed nervously. 'Yeah, I stumbled when I first came to. I guess I got up too quickly and wasn't steady on my feet. I managed to fall backward and clang my head right where I already had the wound.'

Albert didn't argue or try to work out how the man might have managed such a feat. Instead, he went back to the doors. They were a pair that opened in the middle, hence the top and bottom floor bolts to keep them in place once closed. Otherwise the handle in the middle where they met would fail to do the job. Looking at them from outside, it was the right-hand door which had the two bolts on it. He looked at them now, inspecting them critically with his reading glasses on so he could get close and still see fine detail.

Oxford saw the old man on his knees and came over to see what he might have found. 'What've you got, Albert?'

Albert scratched at a mark on the bottom bolt with his thumbnail. Then grabbed the door for support as he tried to get back up.

Oxford saw his struggle and moved in to assist, offering a hand to get Albert back on his feet.

'Thank you, Oxford,' Albert said absentmindedly. His focus was on the top bolt now, where he found the same type of mark as he'd seen on the bottom one. A wild theory began to take shape. PC Shaw moved in to see what might have caught Albert's interest, but Albert turned away. 'I think we should move on. There's nothing to see here.'

The announcement surprised Oxford. 'Oh, really?'

'Yes. It's quite clear that Dave spent the night in the chiller. He's lucky he's not in worse shape after all those hours stuck in the cold. I should think most people would have frozen to death.'

Dave patted his ample belly. 'I have plenty of insulation,' he laughed at his own joke.

Neither Oxford nor Albert gave comment, but Albert called Rex to his side. 'We should get to Filip Fiske's house.'

Make me some Toast, Babe

They dropped Dave back at his house on their way, bidding him goodbye and good luck before pushing on to the address they had for Filip. Oxford ran a check on Mr and Mrs Fletcher during the night when he first found Filip's address. They were the couple who owned the house in which Filip Fiske had been lodging for almost two years. Mr Fletcher was a graphic designer for an engineering firm, and she worked at a secondary school as a history teacher. Together they made a sensible wage, but probably not enough once the mortgage, loan repayments, and bills were paid to allow for any luxuries. Hence the lodger.

They had no criminal record. Not a thing. And no hint that they had any idea what sort of person their lodger was. To be fair, there was no legal demand that a person pay to have a background check before letting a room, and in the two years since he moved in, he hadn't been arrested. One might even be fooled into thinking he had turned a corner in his life.

Oxford and Albert knew differently.

In the quiet of the car, a thought occurred to Albert. 'Have the bodies been identified yet?'

'I don't think so,' replied Oxford while checking his rear-view mirror. 'There's been no bulletin. Why do you ask?'

'It's been more than a day since the bodies were found. They must have worked out who it is by now, especially after speaking with Dave Thornwell. The moment he gave them his Karl Somethingski name, they will have been able to find Karl Tarkovsky, just like you did. We could be about to run into other officers if they have tracked the trail to Filip Fiske's fixed abode.'

'Good point,' Oxford conceded. 'Once they have Karl Tarkovsky's name, it isn't much of a leap to work out who they have in the morgue.'

Albert stayed quiet while Oxford used his phone. It was connected to the car's handsfree equipment, but Albert couldn't understand why he wasn't using the radio to talk with dispatch.

A voice echoed out from the speakers. 'Oxford, is that you?'

'Hi, Megan. Yeah, it's me.' To Albert he whispered, 'We came through training together.'

'You're not coming here, are you?' Megan sounded concerned that he might visit the Peterborough station. 'Your name is mud right now. I overheard those two cows, Patrice and Keeley, laughing about how horrible the chief inspector was to you yesterday. He needs taking down a peg or two. Did you really try to take over his investigation?'

If being talked about bothered him, he brushed it to one side to get to the reason for his call. 'Nevermind all that rubbish. Megan there was a double murder the night before last. Have the bodies been identified yet?'

'No,' she replied without hesitation. 'No. I'm not involved in the case, but I know they haven't got anywhere with it yet. The chief inspector is handling it himself along with his favourites, those two slutbags, Patrice and Keeley. Why do you want to know?' Then she gasped as she worked out the answer to her own question. 'Oh, my goodness, you are trying to take over his investigation! What are you doing, Oxford? He's going to string you up when he finds out!'

Oxford nodded and pursed his lips. 'Yup. Probably. But I know who the two dead men are, and I know why they were killed. I might even have worked out who killed them.' He was exaggerating badly now, but his mouth was running away with itself. 'I just needed to know if anyone there knew. Thanks, Megan. You're a star.'

'I might well be, but you're going to get yourself fired, Oxford. Back away, pretend like you were in Stilton the whole time minding your own business, and maybe the chief won't find out.'

'That's good advice, Megan, thanks. I think though, that I shall solve the whole case, arrest all the bad guys, and get a medal. Make me some toast, babe, I'll be back for breakfast.' He ended the call before she had a chance to speak again. On a massive high, he suddenly realised what he'd said and felt his stomach tighten.

'Make me some toast,' Albert repeated slowly with a wry chuckle. 'I'll be back for breakfast.'

Oxford felt his cheeks redden. 'In my head it sounded like something cool to say.'

Albert smirked again. 'It probably was a cool thing to say. If you pull this off. Otherwise, your friend Megan is going to think you are a big dummy.'

His cheeks went even redder.

Filip Fiske's Room

T he Fletchers lived in Farcet, a suburb of Peterborough to the south of the city. Finding their house was easy enough but there was no great surprise to either man when they were not at home.

Albert leaned on the roof of the car. 'It's lunchtime on a Friday. They might not be back until early evening. Or they might have arranged to meet after work and go straight out for dinner which might mean it's bedtime before they return.'

With a waggle of his eyebrows, Oxford shut his car door and locked it. 'I thought of that. Mrs Fletcher works at Addington Academy,' he pointed down the road, 'which is right there.'

And so it was. Less than a hundred yards from her door was her place of work, making it a very short commute indeed.

Impressed that Oxford had his bases covered, Albert eyed his dog. 'We are going into a school, Rex. You need to behave, understood? No barking at the children, even if they smell of marijuana.'

Rex would have shrugged his indifference if his shoulders worked that way. Since they didn't, he started walking, jerking his human's hand to make him stumble slightly.

There was no security at the school gate as one might find in the big cities, such as London. This is rural England, where the concept of crime in school is laughable. There were a few schoolchildren transitioning between classes; they gave the man in uniform a lingering look, but no one spoke to them until they entered reception.

There were two ladies behind the reception desk; one in her late sixties who most likely knew everything there was to know about the school and who had very possibly been working there since her teenage years. Her name badge declared her name to be Rachel. Sitting just along from her was the woman who Rachel might have been when she first started: a teenager called Jessica. Both women looked up as the men entered the reception area through the large glass doors at the front of the building, their concerned expressions matched as if it were the first time they had ever seen a police officer on the premises.

'Can we be of assistance?' asked Rachel, getting to her feet.

'I need to speak with Mrs Fletcher, please,' said Oxford.

Rachel sounded surprised when she asked, 'That's it?'

Oxford shot a glance at Albert, who could only give him a blank look in return. 'Um, yes. Should there be anything else?'

Rachel sat down again, landing heavily in her chair as if a wave of relief were crashing over her. 'Well, it's just that you read about so many things happening, that when I saw you coming through the door with a sniffer dog ...'

'She thought this was a drugs bust,' Jessica confessed. 'That or a terrorist had planted a bomb in the school and the dog was here to sniff it out before we all got blown to smithereens.'

'It is neither of those things,' Albert attempted to reassure the older woman who even now was fanning her face and puffing from the self-induced excitement. 'This is Rex Harrison. He's my assistance dog.'

'Rex Harrison?' Jessica echoed. 'Wasn't he one of the Beatles?'

Her question was enough to snap Rachel back to reality. 'That's George Harrison. Your general knowledge is terrible, girl. Now get along and send a runner to fetch Mrs Fletcher. Who's she got as her assistant today?'

Jessica took a second to consult her computer. 'Mrs Fairfellow.'

That met with approval from Rachel. 'Good. She'll be able to manage the class while Mrs Fletcher is talking to these gentlemen.'

Whether Mrs Fairfellow could or could not control the class in her absence never once came up in the conversation Mrs Fletcher had with Albert and Oxford, but Filip the lodger did.

'Yes, he didn't come home last night which is most unlike him,' she told them both. They were in a small room, which she called a breakout room, just to the side of reception. 'He's done it before, of course, but only once or twice, and he always appears the next day sober and sensible. Robert, that's my husband,' she added in case they didn't know, 'he thinks he probably just got lucky and will reappear in a few days or whenever he is ready.'

'What does he do for a living?' asked Albert. Oxford had gone for the direct approach, asking her when she last saw him, but Albert was an old hand at this and wanted to ease the lady into revealing everything she knew.

'He works in construction, I think,' she truly didn't sound or look convinced. 'His English isn't good, so we don't exactly talk, but he always pays his rent. We've never had to chase him for it. Whatever he does, it supplies a steady wage, I guess.'

'What makes you think he works in construction?' Albert took what she told him and gave her a follow up question.

'Well,' she started but then stopped as she questioned her own mind. 'I don't know really,' she laughed nervously. 'He comes home dirty quite often. But now that I think about it, it's more like ink than dirt on his clothes and skin. We don't see much of him. He never tries to join us of an evening. Look, I'm sorry, what is this about?'

Ignoring her question, Albert pressed her for more information. 'Did he mention going away?'

'Going away?' she repeated.

'Did he recently pack a bag or a suitcase? Had he mentioned that he might be gone for a short while?'

'No nothing like that. Is he in trouble? Has he done something wrong? I mean, I wouldn't want to think badly of him, but here I am being questioned by the police.' Her face had coloured as her discomfort with the situation began to overwhelm her.

Albert whispered quickly to Oxford, prompting him to advance the conversation. 'Mrs Fletcher, I have reason to believe that Filip Fiske may be in possession of stolen goods and that stolen goods may be stored at your property. I can obtain a search warrant easily enough, but I would rather avoid that if you will accompany me to your premises and allow me to perform a cursory search right now.'

Mrs Fletcher, the history teacher, looked as if she were about to faint. 'Oh, my God. I've been harbouring a criminal. All these years, and ... and ...' her eyes snapped up to look at the two men, wide and disbelieving, she stammered, 'What will this do to my insurance?'

They had to calm her down, which took a few minutes plus a cup of sweet tea, courtesy of Jessica in reception. Once the colour returned to her face and she was better able to rationalise the information, Mrs Fletcher let them know that she had a free period next and more than enough time to take them to her house. She didn't think Filip had packed a suitcase; she certainly hadn't seen one but couldn't rule out that he might have gone away.

Albert and Oxford were convinced he had been murdered but they were not able to deliver that news because the body had yet to be identified.

Mrs Fletcher left a message with reception and had them log her as off-site before leading the two men and a dog back to her house. 'I take it you called here first,' she said, observing the squad car parked in front of her property. Inside, she led them to the room at the back which she rented to Filip. It was neatly decorated in neutral colours and in contrast to Karl's room in Donald's rundown house, it was also neatly kept. The bed was made, the curtains were hung neatly, and there was no visible dust on any of the surfaces. He had a family picture of a younger Filip with his parents and an old dog on a shelf next to a line of books. The titles were in Lithuanian.

'I need to look in the drawers and wardrobe, Mrs Fletcher,' Oxford stated, pausing before he moved so she could give her permission – he had no search warrant after all.

She said simply, 'Please,' and hung around at the doorway to watch.

Rex was in the room, standing by the bed and sniffing - there was nothing interesting to smell. There were plenty of scents for his nose to discern, sort, and decipher, yet nothing out of the ordinary for a human bedroom. There were some mouse droppings somewhere, most likely under the bed where a half-eaten late-night packet of crisps had fallen and been forgotten. Otherwise, the smells were clothing in need of laundry, clothing that had been laundered and a vaping kit in the nightstand next to the single bed.

The wardrobe and drawers, much like the room itself, were neat and organised. The clothes were folded or neatly ironed and hung. Shirts were with shirts, polos were next to the other polos. To make it any more meticulous, Filip would have to arrange by hues of the rainbow.

A small suitcase was on top of the wardrobe. Oxford didn't bother to open it; the act of lifting it a half inch told him it was empty. He poked about in the drawers, Oxford doing all the searching while Albert kept his hands behind his back – the younger man was the one here in an official capacity.

In less than ten minutes, they decided there was nothing to find. It served as a reminder to Albert of just how frustrating police work can be. Finding a whole Stilton in his top drawer with a slice cut from it and an open box of crackers might have been a nice indicator of guilt. However, he wasn't so sure anymore that he expected to find the cheese. It was beginning to look like he'd taken a wrong turn right at the start and dragged poor Oxford along with him.

Standing in Filip's bedroom among belongings he would never return for, Albert accepted the truth that they were running out of leads to follow. They could still check out Flint Lane and they had addresses for the other two known associates, either or both of whom might be Karl and Filip's killer. Whether they all proved to be dead ends too, or perhaps just dead, there was no need to hang on any longer in the Fletchers' house.

With a nudge to get him moving, Albert led Rex back out onto the landing.

Dutifully, Oxford said, 'Thank you for your time and for your assistance, Mrs Fletcher.'

'You still haven't told me what this is about,' she pointed out.

'Filip is wanted with regard to an ongoing enquiry, ma'am, that's all at this time.'

'So, it's nothing to do with funny money, then?'

Her question stopped Albert and Oxford dead in their tracks. They were both heading down the stairs to the front door but froze mid-flight so they could turn around and stare up at her.

'He gave you a counterfeit note?' asked Albert, unable to stop himself from getting the question in before PC Shaw had a chance.

'Twice, actually.' Mrs Fletcher looked relieved to have told someone.

Albert started moving again, arriving in the lower hallway where he paused for the others to join him. When Mrs Fletcher arrived, she squeezed past them to get to her small kitchen. 'I have them in here.'

The kitchen wasn't big enough for all three of them to go inside, necessitating that both men wait at the entrance and watch while Mrs Fletcher took a jar from a cupboard at head height. From the jar, which she set on the counter, she extracted a small white envelope – the type and size most bills arrive in. 'My husband spotted it when he went through the rent money.'

Albert interrupted with a question, 'Does he always pay you cash?'

'Yes. He even paid his deposit in cash when he first moved in. He told us he doesn't trust banks because people can rob them.' The irony of that statement from a known thief made both men smirk.

Oxford took the offered twenty-pound notes and held them up, side by side to the light coming through the kitchen window. The error, which they now knew to look for, was obvious.

Mrs Fletcher continued to talk. 'It was just one note among all the others. We didn't want to make a big deal of it, so we stuffed it out of the way and forgot about it until we got another one this Monday. The first one we figured was a fluke, someone had paid him with a dodgy bank note. You hear about it all the time, but I'd never seen one myself before. Then, when we got the second, we knew we had to say something to him.'

'But you hadn't had that conversation yet?' said Albert, making the question into a statement.

She shook her head. 'No, we were trying to find the right moment.'

You missed your chance, Albert thought to himself.

By his feet, Rex thought, this is a kitchen, why don't we all have a snack?

Oxford handed the notes back. 'You need to hand these to the police, Mrs Fletcher. Thank you for showing us.'

With a frown she pointed out, 'But you are the police.'

'They have to be taken at a station so they can be recorded as evidence and you will need to give a short statement about how you came into their possession.' In truth, he could have done it all, but daylight was running away from them. It was already well after noon, and they had more threads still to follow.

She looked disappointed, but took the notes back, and placed them back into the envelope, then back into the jar, and finally the jar went back into the cupboard. 'I'll do that tomorrow. I need to get back to school now if there's nothing else you need from me.' She glanced out the window as she was announcing her plan to leave the house, something distracting her outside. 'Were you expecting friends?' she asked.

Undercover Sting Op

O xford's heart stopped beating as he watched the chief inspector get out of his squad car and straighten his hat. He was looking directly at the house, and though he wouldn't be able to see Oxford and Albert standing inside it, he clearly knew they were here. Oxford's own squad car parked right out front was enough of a giveaway, but the chief inspector hadn't spotted it by accident - he knew Oxford was here and knew what he was up to.

Flustered, Oxford's jaw flapped up and down a few times as he struggled to find something to say.

Albert came to his rescue. 'Yes, Mrs Fletcher. That's the chief inspector. We ought to go outside and speak with him. Thank you once again for your help today.'

Oxford managed to mumble his thanks as well. His stomach was doing flips and making him feel nauseous. His hands felt like they might start shaking and he had to bite his teeth together and tell himself to get a grip. When he'd calmed some, he stuffed his hat back onto his head, and went outside to face the music.

Albert gripped Oxford's elbow as they closed the distance to where the chief inspector waited patiently – he knew they would come to him and it gave him dominance to patiently await their arrival. When Oxford leaned his head down, Albert whispered, 'It'll be alright, lad. This game isn't played out yet.'

Oxford had no idea what that meant but there was no time to seek clarity because they were at the end of the garden path.

The chief inspector stepped forward and thrust out his right hand for Oxford to shake. 'Well done, PC Shaw. I must say you have truly surprised me.'

Oxford's hand was being pumped up and down though he felt disconnected from it. Bewildered by the turn of events and the chief inspector's new attitude, he couldn't find a thing to say.

The chief inspector released PC Shaw's hand so he could offer a handshake to the old man as well. 'I'm sure I need to congratulate you as well, though I will say that I wish you had both listened to my advice and stayed well away from this.'

'What's going on, sir?' Oxford couldn't bear his confusion any longer.

The sound of a front door closing drew their attention and stilled any further conversation as Mrs Fletcher left her house to return to school. They all stepped out of her way to give her free passage along the pavement and remained silent until she was an appropriate distance away.

The chief inspector sucked in a deep breath through his nose and let it go. 'There is a counterfeiting operation in Peterborough. It has been operating for some time, flooding the country with phoney twenty-pound notes and, until recently, no one knew where it was. The focus of my efforts over the past few months has been in tracking them down. The murder of Filip Fiske and Karl Tarkovsky tipped my hand – I knew I would have to move soon.'

'You know who the bodies are, sir?' Oxford was just getting more confused. 'I thought they hadn't been identified yet.'

The CI nodded. 'Officially they haven't, but I have an undercover operative inside the counterfeiting ring and know who the main players are. I knew who they both were the moment I saw their pictures. I needed a little time to set up a sting operation, but suddenly you were in the way, distracting everyone with a lockup filled with stolen goods and concerns about some cheese. As soon as you started asking questions yesterday, I made a point of monitoring where your car was. As you know, all police cars are fitted with a tracker, so it was easy to see when you went to Mr Tarkovsky's house. I thought perhaps you would exhaust all the leads and give up, but, like your father, you are quite tenacious.'

'Sorry, sir,' Oxford wasn't sure if he was supposed to apologise or not, but it seemed like the right thing to do.

The chief inspector waved him off. 'You were doing your job. I see now that I should have brought you into my confidence. I could have saved myself some work had I done so. I came here to stop you going any further, but now that you know what is going on, I think I should like to reward you.'

'Sir?'

'The bust is due to take place in an hour. How would you like a starring role? You can make the arrests.'

'Sir?'

Albert stayed quiet.

'Well, you've tracked them this far. If I wasn't here to intervene, I dare say you would have tracked them all the way to their operation and arrested them all. Or, more likely, got killed the moment they spotted you.'

Oxford asked, 'Is the counterfeit operation in Flint Lane?'

The chief inspector's eyes flared, and he let out a loud laugh. 'My goodness. Is there anything you haven't worked out yet?'

A confused smile crept onto Oxford's face. He wasn't sure what emotion he was supposed to be feeling. He was being praised for his work and that felt great. The chief inspector was also inviting him to take part in a raid where he would not only get to make his first ever arrest but would be making multiple arrests as they broke up a big organised crime operation. It was medal-winning stuff for a young officer if the CI chose to see it that way and recommend him for an award.

The chief inspector was waiting for Oxford to say something, but the poor young man was still too flabbergasted to respond.

Albert stepped in yet again. 'PC Shaw would like to accept this honour, Chief Inspector. It is most gracious of you to offer it.'

'Yes, most gracious,' agreed Oxford, finally finding his voice.

Albert made himself sound humble when he added, 'I will take this opportunity to apologise for any extra work I may have caused by poking my nose in to help PC Shaw in the pursuit of his duties.'

Again, the chief inspector waved for him to stop. 'Water under the bridge. I am glad we arrived at this place and we should let that be the end of it.' He looked from Albert to Oxford and then back to Albert who he then addressed, 'Now, I think I have a role for you both. That is, sir, if you would like to assist the police in apprehending the crooks you have so doggedly chased since you arrived here yesterday.'

Put on the spot, it wasn't impossible for Albert to decline the offer, but he'd been expecting it and was ready to say yes. 'It would be my honour to serve again,' he said, letting pride swell his chest.

'Amazing.' The chief inspector clapped his hands. 'I have to get back to the station and get ready with the tactical squad commander who will be leading the raid.'

Oxford's brow wrinkled for the hundredth time in the last five minutes. 'I'm not going to be a part of the squad?'

'Goodness, no, PC Shaw. Those men and women train together all the time and are practiced so they know what the person next to them will do in a given situation. No, it would be highly inappropriate for you to join them. I won't be joining them either. I'll be a tactical step behind when they burst through the doors.'

Even more confused, Oxford asked, 'Then where will I be, sir?'

The chief inspector opened the back door of his car, 'I'm glad you asked, PC Shaw.' From the back seat, he produced a street map of Peterborough on which he proceeded to show them the location of the building on Flint Lane, the location of the strike squad and where he would be with the second response unit who would sweep in once the criminals inside had been subdued. 'Our man on the inside tells us they have a lookout on the first floor of the building at all times. I need you, PC Shaw, to distract him. Your presence in the street will draw his eyes to watch you. Make sure you are looking directly at his building and pretend to talk into your radio. Make the lookout nervous so he focusses only on you. You, sir,' he looked at Albert, 'together with your dog. I want you to be a harmless bystander. It will look more natural if there are people in the street, which there otherwise will not be because we will clear it and block off the access routes before we put in the strike.'

'That makes good sense,' agreed Albert with a nod of acknowledgement.

'Thank you. I was going to use a couple of officers from the station, but the pair of you deserve this honour. Just act natural and when you hear the first blast, as the strike team blow a door on the rear of the building, make sure to get clear. There will be officers waiting at the end of the street. That's you, Mr Smith, not you, PC Shaw. When the strike happens, get to my command post. You and I will be going in together. There are some high value criminals in there and they all need to be arrested.'

Oxford was so excited by the sudden change in fortune, he could barely contain his excitement. 'What time, sir? What time do you need us there?'

The chief inspector rolled the street map back up. 'Four o'clock sharp. Synchronise watches.' Both police officers held up their wrists, Oxford resetting his so the time matched exactly when the chief inspector called it. 'You have less than an hour, gentlemen. I must return to the station and prepare. Good luck. I'll see you there. Do not be late, PC Shaw.'

'No, sir. Thank you, sir. You can count on me, sir.'

Albert tipped his head in a slight salute to the senior officer and watched him slide back into his car. Once it vanished from sight, Albert took out his phone and made a call. While he waited for it to connect, he watched Oxford bouncing with excitement. He wondered how long it would take for the lad to ask the obvious question. As it turned out, it wasn't long at all.

Oxford stopped bouncing when a random thought entered his head. Completely caught up in the raid he was about to take part in, and thoughts of being able to talk about it in the pub later, the singular purpose for his day had escaped him. Locking eyes with Albert, he asked, 'What does any of this have to do with the missing cheese?'

Ill-thought Ideas

The stallholders ought to have been set up by late morning and be selling their wares to early arrivals in the village by early afternoon. A few were, but the bulk were too concerned about the lack of Stilton to continue working. The dairy workers especially, truck drivers, cheesemakers, quality inspectors, and a myriad other roles were employed to put up signs, erect bunting and sweep the street clean in preparation for the big weekend.

Management were nowhere in sight, and middle-management weren't sure they didn't agree with the general murmuring going around the village.

Tom wanted to know, 'Why am I supposed to be cleaning the road signs and digging weeds out of the gutters if there is no Stilton? What's the point?' He'd been moaning for hours, but not without result. Many others felt exactly the same as he did, they just weren't vocalising it as loudly.

Hugh Stephens, the transport manager and Tom's immediate boss, came over to speak with him. 'Now, Tom, we've no reason to believe the festival won't go ahead. I think we should all think about our jobs and how we can help the dairy recover from the theft.'

'Was the cheese really stolen?' asked a new voice, that of Lenny Ditton, the town's baker and all-round barrack room lawyer. 'I bet it's not been stolen at all. I bet they've hidden it.'

'Why on Earth would they do that?' snorted Hugh incredulously, looking around at the faces taking interest in their conversation and expecting support.

'To drive up the price,' Lenny replied. 'Make a commodity scarce and the price goes up. Everyone knows that. If it was stolen, you can bet the dairy shareholders are behind it.'

Silence followed his statement for a two count, then conspiracy theories exploded from every direction as years of disgruntlement from a small selection of employees began to infect those around them.

Tom looked at his hands. They were dirty. He had grime under his fingernails and muck on his clothes. He doubted Mr Brenner, the dairy's managing director, ever got dirt under his fingernails. By his feet, the bucket of weeds he dug out already laughed up at him, mocking his hard work because it would never get him anywhere.

When he kicked it viciously across the street, all conversation stopped and he looked around at the people he knew. 'I've had enough,' he growled. 'Stuff the dairy management and the shareholders. I'm going for a pint. Who's with me?'

Nervous Times

I n the car on their way to Peterborough, Albert explained a few things to Oxford. He wasn't certain he had it right until his phone rang and he got a rather excited answer back. A short argument followed, which neither party won, yet his request would be met and that was good enough.

When the call ended, he put his phone on his lap and chuckled to himself. 'There's nothing like handing people a tight timeline and challenging them to meet it.'

'Will this work?' asked Oxford.

'Absolutely,' Albert lied.

On Cross Street, just around the corner from Flint Lane, Oxford parked his squad car and locked it. Now that the raid was about to take place, a squadron of butterflies were doing acrobatics in his stomach. Trainee officers got to practice scenarios like this at the academy, but that was in a benign environment where they could make it as exciting as they liked because they knew no one was going to really get hurt. This was entirely different, especially when one added in the changes to the chief inspector's plan that Albert insisted were necessary. Of course, Oxford had been privy to the call Albert placed, it came through on speakerphone in a kaleidoscope of revelation he would never have been able to imagine for himself.

He knew the truth and now he had to see his investigation through to the end. He doubted he had ever been more terrified.

He glanced around the corner of a building and into Flint Lane. It was devoid of people as the chief inspector said it would be. Albert had taken Rex and circled around so they could both come into the street from separate ends. They would act casual so as not to tip anyone off, least of all the counterfeiters' lookout somewhere above them looking down.

At 1558hrs Oxford started walking. Albert appeared at the other end of the street, roughly three hundred yards away. They would converge about a third of the way along from Albert's end, Oxford walking faster to make up the extra distance.

His pulse hammered in his head as he continued onward doing exactly as instructed by the chief inspector as he looked at the buildings. Eyeing them critically, he felt certain the lookout would have spotted him coming by the time he was halfway along the street. Was he relaying word of the approaching cop to others inside the building?

Behind Albert, two men came into the street. Oxford saw them, and though they were expected, it still made his heart tap a staccato beat. He didn't look back at the street behind him for he felt certain there would be men there too.

More men appeared behind Albert, all of them looking to be filled with menacing purpose. There were no weapons visible but that didn't mean they weren't carrying them concealed inside their jackets.

The premises along Flint Lane appeared to have gone out of business some time ago, just as Oxford described. Signs above the doors and windows were dirty or broken, the windows themselves were closed off by thick steel grates, but some had been broken by determined vandals, nevertheless.

Albert and Oxford were fifty yards apart. Now thirty. Now ten. They both slowed as they reached the address where Karl had parked his car and been ticketed by an overzealous traffic warden. It could have been any of the doors along this section of the street, but they knew they had the right one because the chief inspector confirmed the address an hour ago.

Oxford's hands were sweaty, he noticed, as he clenched and opened them to get rid of the pins and needles which was also probably a symptom of the nerves he felt. There were now six men behind Albert, each of them looking as rough as the others, and when he stole a glance over his shoulder finally, he counted six more behind him. With a jolt of surprise, he realised that he recognised two of them: Darius Balthis and Jokubas Kaleckas were behind him, herding him toward the building where the chief inspector said the counterfeiters were working.

They'd walked into a trap.

Grinding to a halt right in front of a nondescript door that led into the address the chief inspector gave them, Oxford gave Albert a nervous smile and got a confident nod in return.

Then the door opened inwards and from the dark came a familiar face.

Raid

'Welcome, gentlemen,' said the chief inspector. 'You look a little surprised to see me.'

Oxford's jaw was on the floor or would have been were it not attached to his face. 'Sir, what's going on? What about the raid? Did we miss it?'

A smile broke out on the senior officer's face, which he shared with the rough men now surrounding Albert and Oxford. Then it vanished from sight, replaced by a mean scowl as he said, 'Get them.'

Oxford got to watch the chief inspector go back inside the building, disappearing into the darkness inside, but had no time to react for he was being grasped by multiple hands and driven forward toward the door.

Albert shouted, 'Don't fight them, lad. It'll only go worse if you fight.'

'Listen to the old man,' growled a heavily accented voice right next to his left ear and with that, he was plunged through the dread portal and into the gloom.

Even though Oxford didn't fight, one of the men thought it would be a good idea to incentivise good behaviour by landing a few hard punches to his kidneys. As he twisted to get away from the pain, another joined in the fun by punching him in the gut. Now doubled over and choking for breath, he couldn't resist when they threw him roughly to the floor.

Albert landed next to him, sprawling across the dirt as his old body failed to resist the inertia. Oxford did his best to help him to his knees where they both stayed, side by side, staring up at the chief inspector's back. He was still in uniform, looking oddly out of place among the criminal hoodlums he ought to be arresting.

Glancing around, both Oxford and Albert saw they were in a wide space. Whatever the original purpose of the building had been, it was long forgotten; every scrap of equipment or furniture stripped out to leave nothing but bare walls and a grimy floor. However, behind the chief inspector, a dozen expensive-looking and technical electronic devices were steadily making twenty-pound notes. It made surprisingly little noise. The room stretched into the dark on both sides, the only lights those immediately above them. Ten yards behind the machines, a wall hid what might be beyond the single door they could see in it.

The chief inspector took his time, savouring the moment sadistically until he was ready to turn around and face his captives. 'You should have done as I ordered.' He wagged a finger at Oxford. 'Your death today is your own fault. It's not so hard, is it? Following orders? I'm a chief inspector, you are a constable. I say, you do. Simple. So, you'll get no sympathy from me.'

'Is this what happened to Karl and Filip?' asked Albert, confident he already knew the answer. 'Did Karl steal a bunch of notes with an obvious error on them?' When the chief inspector's face twitched, Albert nodded to himself. 'Yes, I figured it was something like that. You had a run of notes with an error but had made millions of pounds worth by the time it was spotted. They were no good, so you gave Karl the job of destroying them. Only he didn't. He told you he did, but secretly, he stashed them. He probably had a plan to leave the country or something, we'll never know because he couldn't resist the temptation to use them. He bought himself a few things, clothes and such, and the notes went into circulation where they were spotted and soon worked their way back to you. You instantly knew who was to blame so you had your ...' Albert glanced at the hard men staring down at him, 'associates cut him into pieces. Was Filip also guilty? Or guilty by association?'

The chief inspector shrugged. 'He claimed to have no knowledge, but I don't like loose ends and I cannot abide stupidity. Karl was being well paid and would have received a bonus shortly, much as these gentlemen have. Like you say, he got greedy and almost ruined the whole thing. Tomorrow, I shall lead an enquiry into PC Shaw's mysterious death. It will most likely make national news, his death that is. It's not often a police officer gets killed in this country but carved up into pieces in the police cottage in Stilton, well, that will be a headline. It will tarnish my career that I never solve it, but hey ho. I guess I'll get by. As for you, Mr Smith, you are just going to vanish. Mourned by your children if you have any, but otherwise soon forgotten.'

There being nothing more to say on the matter, the chief inspector nodded to the men surrounding the captives. It was time to get it done and he was already turning away; he didn't wish to see what the men were going to do.

'Forgetfulness,' said Albert loudly, giving pause to everyone in the room. The chief inspector raised his hand to stay his men before they started the butchery and Albert seized his moment. 'Overconfidence too, but definitely forgetfulness. That is what you will remember as the thing that brought you down.'

Squinting his eyes, the chief inspector glared at the old man. 'What are you talking about? I haven't forgotten anything. No one can touch me because I am the one investigating my own crimes. My system is perfect.'

Albert nodded, his face a mask of sympathetic agreement. 'You, ah ... you don't remember that I had a dog with me before though, do you?' Albert watched as the chief inspector jolted in shock, the memory of the giant dog suddenly at the front of his brain. Revelling in the moment, Albert nevertheless couldn't hesitate and savour it. 'Sic' em, Rex!'

His shout echoed off the ceiling of the room they were in, reverberating as it dissipated and died away, but it was replaced by a bark and the sound of claws running across the concrete floor. The rough men started to look around, but the sound appeared to be coming from everywhere.

The chief inspector needed less than a second to recover from the shock of the old man's outburst. 'Really? One dog? You think he can save you?'

Oxford turned his head to Albert. 'How did I do? Was I convincingly terrified?'

Albert cackled. 'Kid, you could have won an Oscar. The look of surprise when the chief inspector stepped out of the door ... well, I almost believed you weren't expecting to see him.'

'What?' snapped the chief inspector. 'You weren't expecting to see me,' he stated with confidence. 'You had no idea I was behind any of it.' As the bark echoed again, it was joined by another, and then another and the smile faded from the chief inspector's face along with his confidence.

'You see, Chief Inspector,' said Albert, 'the moment you turned up alone at Mrs Fletcher's house, I knew it had to be you. No chief inspector drives his own car. You were alone because you couldn't have anyone seeing what you were doing.'

Rex burst out of the shadows. He was running full tilt, his coat flexing in glorious ripples as he flew across the floor. To his left and right, and then from the opposite direction entirely, more German Shepherd dogs appeared, all sprinting toward their targets and utterly unstoppable.

'You should have checked on me, Chief Inspector. My children are all serving senior police officers.' Albert had to shout over the noise of the dogs barking and the men panicking. The rough men no longer looked frightening. Rather, they looked frightened, and were bumping into each other as they tried to get away from the canine menace heading their way. 'It only took one phone call to my daughter to prove there was no tactical squad arranged in Peterborough. There was never a raid planned, but guess what?' Albert left a pause so the chief inspector could hear the pain-filled yells as the first of his men were taken down by the huge dogs. 'There is now!'

Behind them, the door from the street burst open, and a heavily armed tactical squad poured through it with their assault rifles up. The dog handlers were racing along behind the canines from the left and right, half a dozen of them all moving in to place the counterfeiters under arrest.

Oxford had leapt to his feet the moment the dogs began their attack. He meant to arrest the chief inspector but in all the confusion, he was forced to tackle one of the henchmen. There were more men than there were dogs, so some were going to escape, and he was doing his part. Somehow, though, he'd picked the biggest, strongest, and meanest of them and was having a serious scuffle until he got lucky with an arm hold and was able to subdue him. Stripped of his cuffs, torch, radio, and baton the moment they were grabbed, he now had the man pinned to the floor with a knee while he waited for the armed cops to move in. He could still read the man his rights and claim his first arrest though, so that was what he did.

'You are under arrest on suspi ...' Albert whacked him on the arm.

'Forget him, lad! The chief inspector just legged it!' Albert was already going after him, hurrying along as fast as his legs would go. 'Rex! To me,' he shouted.

Oxford wouldn't have been able to work out which dog was which in the confusion. There was so much growling and screaming going on, it was like attending a werewolf party where the guests ate the hosts. Throw in shouted orders from the tactical squad and several shots that were fired in the enclosed space to stop people escaping, it was no wonder the chief inspector – still in his uniform - had been able to slip away. Nevertheless, when he saw a dog spit out his victim and race after Albert, he knew the three of them had to finish this together.

'Stay here, sir,' he growled at the man beneath his knee. 'I apologise for this break in your arrest service; however, someone will be with you shortly to complete the task.'

The man responded with an outrushing of air from his lungs as Oxford used his knee to push off the floor. Leaping over another officer as he or she made their arrest, Oxford ran after Albert and through the door in the wall behind the machines. It led to a corridor where he had to pause and listen to work out which way to go. To his right, he could hear the old man and his dog ahead of him.

Sprinting, through a right turn and then a left, he suddenly found a bright rectangle of light ahead and burst through it to find himself back in daylight. Albert was ten yards ahead and Rex twenty yards beyond him, sprinting for all he was worth to catch the chief inspector. He was going to make it easily, that is until the chief inspector stopped an elderly man in his car, tore him from the driver's seat and dove inside.

Rex hit the car a heartbeat after the door slammed shut with the chief inspector inside. He was having such a great day! People to chase, people to bite, lots of other dogs around. It was brilliant fun! However, the latest target his human told him to bite was now inside a car and no matter how much he barked at him through the windscreen, he just wouldn't come out to play.

Oxford saw what happened and reacted. Call it blind luck, call it serendipity; whatever the case, his squad car was fifty yards away: they'd come out on Cross Street and the one thing the men inside hadn't taken from him were the keys in his pocket.

'Albert!' His shout reached the old man's ears, spinning him around just as he plipped the car open. It was facing the wrong way, but a furious wheel spin later, he was leaving a month's worth of rubber behind as he powered up the road to collect Albert.

Standing on the bonnet of the car, Rex fell when the human inside selected reverse and slammed the accelerator down. He landed awkwardly but bounced to his feet and gave chase.

Inside the car, the chief inspector was driven by anger and disbelief that an idiot of a constable and a stupid old man had ruined his plans. His only goal now was escape, but the damned dog was chasing him. He wanted to run it over. All he would have to do was slam on his brakes and change direction. Car versus dog: an easy win. His mind got changed for him when the very constable he'd just been cursing, appeared in his squad car. He was a quarter of a mile down the road but coming fast. With a flick of the steering wheel, the chief inspector switched from reverse to forward, throwing the car's front end around in a tight arc and blasting forward. Except it didn't blast forward. He'd stolen the first car that came along, the old man at the wheel stopping because a police officer instructed him to.

It was a Nissan Micra, the bastion of old person cars and about as powerful as a hairdryer. He needed a BMW M5 and a full tank of gas. Cursing his bad luck, he knew he had money stashed away; enough to make the rest of his life very comfortable. All he had to do was get to the coast and escape. With nothing to lose, he goaded the car into giving him all it had and flew through the back streets of Peterborough.

High Speed Pursuit

With a screech of brakes, Oxford stopped the car for Albert to get in, then pumped the pedal to leave yet more rubber on the tarmac as he sped onwards.

Then, he hit the brakes again, throwing Albert forward before he could get his seatbelt on. The old man the chief inspector ripped from his car was getting up off the road. There was a rip in the knee of his trousers.

'Are you alright, sir?' yelled Oxford, adrenalin making him do everything at maximum volume.

Hobbling a little, he stared in through Oxford's open window. 'That police man just took my car. What's going on?'

'Get in, sir,' smiled the young constable, 'and strap in. This is a high-speed pursuit.'

Gamely, the old man settled in behind the driver and waved to Albert, 'Hi, I'm Earnest Toomey. This is an odd sort of occurrence, isn't it? I do hope that police officer won't damage my sister's car. Only I told her I would get it back without a scratch. She's quite precious about it.'

Once he heard the seatbelt click into place, Oxford smashed the gas pedal yet again, but he already knew he had one more passenger to pick up.

Rex ran after the car for as long as he could, but he accepted there were limitations to how fast he could run. Humans liked to cheat; that was the problem. They couldn't outrun dogs, so they built machines to do it for them. When he lost sight of the car, he slowed to get his breath back and sat to wait: his human would be along soon.

He was right too, the very next car contained his human, and the young human they'd spent the last two days with, plus a new human who looked thoroughly surprised and not even slightly happy when Rex bounded into the backseat and gave his face an excited lick.

With the lights flashing and the siren blaring, Oxford tore through the backstreets of Peterborough. The chief inspector was nowhere in sight but that wasn't stopping him.

'There's only one decent way out of the city from where we are,' he explained. 'He'll take the B1091 away from the city to get to the A1(M). From there he can go anywhere and will be much harder to find. I need to call this in.'

He jabbed a button on his steering wheel to activate the in-car radio. 'Dispatch this is Foxtrot Three Zero, over.'

A man's voice came back, 'Dispatch.'

'I am in pursuit of a black Nissan Micra, registration plate ...' he glanced at the old man on the back seat and clicked his fingers to prompt him.

The old man pulled a face. 'Oh, ah, I don't know actually. It's my sister's car. I just borrowed it because my wife and I are visiting and ...'

Oxford cut him off; he didn't have time for the story. 'Nevermind dispatch. I'm on the B1091 heading south doing a hundred and five. Send all units to intercept.'

'Foxtrot Three Zero, be advised all units are currently converging on a developing situation in Flint Lane. There was a raid there in the last half an hour. It looks like the chief inspector caught the counterfeiters.' Albert and Oxford could hear the joy in the man's voice. He hadn't been able to take part, but he'd played his role in coordinating units and had no idea the chief inspector was currently the county's most wanted man.

'That's good news,' said Oxford, with an ironic chuckle. 'Foxtrot Three Zero out.'

'Looks like we are on our own,' Albert observed. 'Tractor ahead.'

The B1091 is the road that links Peterborough and Stilton and is an almost straight line between the two. This was the fifth or sixth time – Albert had lost count – that he had travelled it in the last two days. He was going a mite faster this time.

Oxford had to slow for traffic continually, pushing the boundaries of what was sensible but not going so far as to endanger life. Unless he was wrong about the chief inspector's flight route, they were going to catch up to him soon. The question was whether they would get to him before he reached the motorway. Once there, he could go either way and it became a coin flip to determine if they could catch him at all.

Mob Rules

I n the garden of the Ship Inn, Tom downed the dregs of his fifth pint and decided he'd had enough. Enough of management lying to them, enough of being told what to do by other people, and very much enough of no one doing anything about the stolen cheese. He didn't believe that there was no cheese left at the dairy. It stood to reason that they would keep a reserve in case of emergencies.

'I'm going to make them give it to us!' he announced loudly, standing up to make sure everyone saw him as well as heard him.

'Give what to us?' asked Mark.

Tom burped and replayed the conversation in his head. Realising he'd skipped a whole segment where he explained what he was talking about, he rewound and started again. 'They've got a secret stash of Stilton at the dairy,' he assured the listening crowd. 'They don't want us to have it. This is their way of keeping us down. I bet the Stilton wasn't stolen at all. I bet they just hid it.' He looked around for support and he got it.

'Yeah! I think we should go down there and demand they hand it over,' said Lenny, the barrack room lawyer, as he stood to join Tom. It had been his suggestion that the cheese was hidden to help the stockholders make more money.

Another man joined in. John was a stall holder in town for the weekend with his wife and two brothers. They made a range of pickles which went very well with Stilton and they made a killing at the festival every year. It went terribly by itself though and with Christmas coming up fast, he didn't feel like losing money this weekend. 'I bet this is just so they can drive the price up.'

'Everyone knows a shortage causes a price hike,' agreed Lenny, driving home the only point he had.

By the time they left the pub garden five minutes later, there were thirty-six of them. All in various stages of inebriation, and all convinced the dairy management was hiding the cheese to maximise profit. Marching through the village, they became easy to spot because more and more people joined in. When they reached the High Street, where some stallholders were still hanging around and wondering what to do, their numbers swelled and soon there were more than a hundred increasingly angry people heading to the dairy.

It was a mob, with all the mindless mentality a group of people can possess.

He's Heading for Stilton!

Oxford killed the sirens and lights. He'd been desperate to use them for the last twelve months, desperate to have a high-speed pursuit and feel like a real police officer, but now it was out of his system and he wanted to be able to sneak up on the chief inspector if he could. They were three miles from the motorway. He either got him soon, or he wouldn't get him at all, so he pushed the car even harder, creeping the speed up to a hundred and twenty-five when they found an open patch of road.

Ahead of them and going as fast as his little car would go, the chief inspector could have sworn he saw flashing lights a moment ago. They were way back in the distance, but his foot was to the floor and the car was still only doing eighty-six. Worse yet, whenever he had to slow down because he couldn't get around the car or truck in front, it then took the car ages to get back up to speed.

'Is that it?' Albert squinted through the windscreen.

Oxford squinted too. It was evening now, the sun fading fast to their right to cast long shadows across the countryside in a way that a poet might romanticise. 'It might be,' he murmured.

'How far to the motorway?'

'No more than a mile.' Oxford's shoulders were beginning to ache from gripping the steering wheel too tightly, but he wasn't letting up now. They were close, and thirty seconds later, they knew they had him.

'Hit the noise button, kid,' rasped Albert, chuckling to himself as he had more fun than he could remember in years.

With his left hand, Oxford flicked the switches and filled the air with flashing lights and a wailing siren that startled the driver in front.

Cursing loudly, the chief inspector twitched the steering wheel as they caught him by surprise. He was moments away from slowing down for the roundabout that would take him onto the motorway. Moments away from escape and he'd been planning his next move. They would expect him to go south so he was going to double bluff them and do exactly that, but he wouldn't stay on the A1(M), he would go down a couple of junctions and come off to travel across country via all the back roads until he reached the bigger M1 and then he would go north.

Now he could do none of those things. The only thing preventing the youthful officer behind him from stopping him right this very second was the narrow confines of the road and the barrage of traffic heading home from their day at work. With yet another curse, he refused to slow at the roundabout and flew through a tiny gap to gain a few precious seconds.

Oxford had to stop. It was that or drive head on into the side of an eighteen-wheeler carrying a bulldozer. No lights or sirens were going to get that out of the way, but he forced his way through the traffic the moment its tail cleared his nose and set off after the Nissan once again.

'He's heading into Stilton!' exclaimed Earnest from the back seat. 'That's why we are up here, actually. My wife and I are rather partial to the cheese and there's a festival tomorrow, did you know?'

He got no reply as both cars careened over the roundabout, down the B1043, and into the outskirts of the town. The chief inspector was still doing more than seventy in what was now a thirty limit, and heading for speed bumps intended to ensure drivers behaved in the quiet setting.

The first launched him skyward and in the car behind, Oxford yelled, 'Hang on to something!' as they too bounced over the concrete lump and into the air.

Outside the dairy, the mob was jeering for the management inside to come out and answer for their crimes. 'We want the cheese!' Tom yelled at the top of his lungs.

'And we want it now!' the mob chanted in response.

'We want the cheese!' he repeated.

'And we want it now!'

Inside, Mr Brenner buttoned up his jacket and checked the time on his grandfather's fob watch. His family had run the dairy for six generations, and he wasn't about to be intimidated by an unruly rabble of drunken dairy workers and misguided stallholders who he could easily replace in time for next year's festival.

'I'm not sure going out there is a good idea,' said Mrs Graves, peering around the window frame at the angry people outside.

'Staying inside would be a cowardly option, Cecelia. I am sure the threat of dismissal for our staff will be enough to disperse them. The stallholders will drift away when the numbers in the mob begin to deplete.' Then he beckoned to the rest of the dairy management. 'Come now. A show of solidarity and strength in numbers is called for.'

No one wanted to go outside with him. He hadn't let them go home for two days as they explored and exhausted every avenue trying to solve the Stilton crisis, and Mr Brenner had been calling the chief inspector for an update all afternoon, though he hadn't been able to get through at any point.

Despite Mr Brenner's determination, the rest of the Board agreed there was no point in carrying on. The cheese was gone, and the secret was out. Everyone knew, so it was time to come clean and deal with the aftermath. They would have to refund the stallholders and issue a statement apologising to all the visitors in the area solely for the festival. Then they would start planning for next year. Mr Brenner refused to listen to their pleas, assuring them that all was not lost until it was lost.

As they filed out the Board room door and made their way to the exit to face the rabble outside, a quarter of a mile away, two cars skidded around the corner of North Street and into Church Road. They were going far too fast for the road conditions and both narrowly missed parked cars on the far side as they fought for traction on the tarmac.

'Hey look, there's Dave,' said Oxford, spotting the dairy's security guard on the corner of Fen Lane as they shot by him.

Albert nodded but didn't say anything. Holding the edge of the seat and the handle above his head as he tried to hold on.

Despite the intensity of their situation, Oxford chose to ponder, 'I wonder where he is going?'

It was a rhetorical question, but Albert had an answer. 'I'll tell you later, lad. Just focus on the driving, please.'

The chief inspector was running out of ideas. He needed to lose the chase car with that idiot Shaw in it. Only then could he ditch this car for something more suitable and slip quietly away. He wasn't as familiar with Stilton as he was many other villages in the area. From his perspective as a police officer, nothing interesting ever happened here, but he knew the next turning on the left would take him past the dairy. It had a low wall and no cars parked in front of it ever. Maybe if he timed it right, he could clip the other car and send it into the wall. The road then carried on straight out of the village and into the countryside where the dark would hide him.

It was the best plan he had, so with a huff of breath, he slammed on his brakes and yanked the steering wheel around.

Pulling alongside on his left with the intention of tipping his back end, Oxford overshot and saw the chief inspector whip behind him and into Glebe Street. He cursed, braked, and burned rubber to back up.

It worked better than expected, the chief inspector laughed to himself. He'd given himself a two-hundred-yard gap. He would hide in the next junction and T-bone the squad car as it came by. He thought all that as he looked in his rear-view mirror and waited for the squad car to reappear. Maybe it was more than two hundred yards, but when he flicked his eyes back to the front, he screamed in shock. There was a crowd of people filling the street!

Their terrified faces flashed for a second in his headlights, before he twisted the wheel to avoid hitting them. Out of control, he bounced up the kerb, lifted the front end of the car and sailed over the low wall bordering the dairy.

Mr Brenner, flanked by the rest of the dairy's Board members, were coming out of the door when they heard a roar of engine and a clang of metal on stone.

Tom had been just about to start throwing some handy stones he'd found when the car launched itself over the wall. It hung in the air for what felt like a minute as a hundred faces watched its passage through the air.

Then it slammed into the tarmac with a spray of sparks, bounced once, and barrelled through the front of the dairy's management building. An explosion of bricks, dust, and bits of glass were jettisoned outwards and roofing tiles fell to the ground as the engine coughed and died.

No one said anything. If a flatulent bat had flown by overhead, a person with perfect pitch could have named the note its bottom made, it was that quiet.

Until the roar of another car's engine filled the air.

All eyes shifted focus from the hole in the wall to the new car as it skidded to a stop in front of the dairy. Like something from an action movie, Oxford came out of the squad car at a sprint, leaping the bonnet as he tore toward the hole in the front of the dairy.

The chief inspector emerged from the hole, covered in dirt and brick dust. He had a cut to his chin and another to his forehead and he looked insanely mad like a demon rising from the ashes of the Earth.

Oxford punched him in the mouth.

'Boom!' cackled Albert, also out of the car and hobbling after his young friend.

The chief inspector went over backward, bumped his head on the rear of the Nissan Micra and lay still. He was out for the count.

Rex walked over to sniff him. The last command his human gave him was to chase and stop this human. That instruction remained extant, so far as Rex was concerned, yet it felt unsporting to bite the man now that he was unconscious. As a compromise, he turned sideways and lifted a leg instead.

'Whaaaaa! Get off, get off!' wailed the chief inspector as warm liquid hit his head. He waved a hand to get up and got rewarded with warm liquid on that too.

Rex danced out of the way as the human started to flail his arms angrily, but he needed to make room for the young human anyway.

Yanking free the set of cuffs on the chief inspector's belt, Oxford straddled his boss and clamped his right wrist with the first steel loop. 'You are under arrest on suspicion of murder,' he recited with a gleeful look on his face. 'You do not have to say anything, but it may harm your defence if you do not mention when questioned something which you later rely on in court. Anything you do say may be given in evidence.' With a yank, he hauled the chief inspector upright. 'Did I get that about right, sir? Looks like I bagged a decent first arrest after all.'

Albert couldn't stop his grin or make it go away. His back hurt from getting thrown around in the car, his shoulders still ached from Rex yanking them earlier when Tom threatened Mrs Graves, and he seemed to have missed both lunch and dinner. But he felt jubilant beyond belief.

'What the heck is this?' asked a slightly slurry voice from his left.

Albert turned to find Tom, the idiot from earlier, swaying at the leading edge of a crowd of people. He had some rocks in his hand and an angry frown dominating his brow. 'Rex, to me, please.'

Rex trotted across to stand at his human's side.

Albert locked eyes with Tom, refusing to break his gaze until the other man blinked. Then he looked at the men and women standing behind him. He was buying time. This was Oxford's village, and Albert would leave him to deal with it.

Oxford could see the crowd and he knew most of the people by name. He had to kick Earnest out of the back seat. He'd found himself trapped there, since the back doors of police cars are not supposed to be opened from the inside and unlike Rex, he wasn't athletic or flexible enough to dart between the front seats. Once the space was empty, Oxford reversed his suspect inside and secured him. 'Sit tight, chief inspector. I'll be back soon. I have a little more policing to do, it would seem.' Then he yanked the senior officer's radio free and took it with him. 'I might need some back up, don't you think?' he explained with a smile.

The Cheese

Joining Albert where he stood between the rabble and the dairy management, Oxford assessed the situation quickly and focused on the man standing apart from the crowd. Unbeknownst to Tom, when Albert and Rex singled him out, those close behind him had all shuffled back a few feet, distancing themselves from the ringleader because they wanted to be able to claim that they'd just followed a crowd: they weren't even sure what was going on. Honest.

'What are you doing, Tom?' Oxford's question carried authority, something Albert hadn't heard in the lad's voice a day ago.

'This doesn't concern you,' Tom slurred. 'This is between us, the people, and those management types who want to keep us in our place. They've hidden the cheese to drive up the price and I demand to know why!' He managed to sound convincing and he got a half-hearted ripple of approval from the rabble.

Mr Brenner stepped forward to answer the accusation. 'Thank you, young Oxford, I ...'

'Constable,' Oxford interrupted.

'I'm sorry?' Mr Brenner didn't follow and wasn't used to being interrupted.

'You addressed me as young Oxford. Young is not a rank. I am this village's police officer. You may address me as Constable Shaw or Officer Shaw, either is acceptable.'

Mr Brenner's face became thunder. It was one thing to have the staff revolt, but he wasn't going to be spoken down to by a young upstart still wet behind the ears with half the village watching. 'Now just you wait a moment, young man.'

'That's not a very polite way to speak to a police officer, now is it, Mr Brenner? Shall I expect you to always be this disrespectful? I note that the righthand headlight on your Bentley isn't working, sir. I was going to speak to you about it, but events of the day have somewhat overtaken me. Shall we talk about that now, or should I issue a fine and move on to more important matters?'

'Well, I ah. I was going to get that done in the morning. Running the dairy is a very time-consuming role I'll have you know.'

Albert stepped up behind Oxford to whisper a few words. They needed to act swiftly now.

With a smile at Mr Brenner, Oxford said, 'Be sure that you do it tomorrow, Mr Brenner. Now be quiet, there's a good gentleman.' While shock spread across the dairy managing director's face, Oxford addressed everyone present. 'The Stilton was stolen. But it hasn't left the village yet. If you would like to follow me, I think it is probably time we got it back.'

He didn't give them a chance to ask questions, he spun on his heel and started back along Glebe Street on foot. Once out of earshot, he whispered to Albert, 'Are you sure about this?'

Albert had been running scenarios through his head all day, ever since he first spotted the possibility of the truth.

'Do you think my sister's car is going to be driveable?' asked Earnest, popping up in front of them. 'Only, she's probably wondering where I am.'

In all the excitement, they'd forgotten all about the poor man the chief inspector carjacked. 'Right,' said Oxford decisively. 'Come with me, sir. I have a small matter to deal with, but I will arrange for someone to get you home. I'm afraid the car isn't going anywhere but your sister will be compensated.'

Earnest fell into step behind the two men and the dog as the rest of the rabble, and the dairy management, all followed him.

'Where are we going?' Mr Brenner demanded to know.

'Fen Lane,' Albert shouted back so everyone would hear.

More questions followed, but neither man answered them. The procession wound its way along Church Road to the corner where a few minutes ago Oxford and Albert had two wheeled the squad car to make the turning out of North Road. This time they continued directly across the street to the mouth of Fen Lane where a set of headlights were coming toward them.

Albert and Oxford simply stopped walking, letting the crowd catch them and form a blockade with their bodies. There was no way out of Fen Lane unless the driver wanted to plough through them all. When there was enough to fill the street from side to side, they started forward again. Murmuring rippled through the crowd as conjecture and conspiracy theories ebbed and flowed.

The truck stopped when it first saw the people filling the street and the driver sighed a defeated sigh. He switched off the engine and waited.

Flicking the radio to loud-speaker mode, Oxford held it to his lips. 'Come on out, Dave. It's over. We know everything.'

With another dejected huff, Dave opened the door and got out. He'd come so close. This was his village. He'd grown up here but when he got out of jail, he'd never be able to return. That was assuming the buyer let him live.

When Oxford and the old man with the dog approached him with the crowd right on their heels, he had to ask, 'How did you catch me?'

Albert snorted a quiet laugh. 'It was coincidence. You had a story planned, didn't you? Steal all the cheese, load it into a truck and hide it in a lockup in the village. You couldn't leave Stilton because the next village is miles away and you had to get back to the dairy so you would be found trapped on the premises the next morning. You wanted people to believe you couldn't have stolen it because you were the one they overpowered and locked inside. Unfortunately, you made a bunch of mistakes.'

The crowd fanned out, some of them stopping to listen to the tale, but others rushing to the back of the truck to check inside. A jubilant shout of, 'It's here! All the cheese is here!' was greeted by a cheer, but Albert continued his story.

'There was no blood on the floor where you said they hit you on the head. Your wound required several stitches and head wounds always bleed badly. Rex would have found the blood instantly, his nose is always drawn to it, but he found nothing. That wasn't definitive, but there was blood in the chiller. You told us you hit your head on the shelf when you came to, but that's where you chose to hit your head to inflict the wound so you could claim to have been attacked. You went into the chiller and should have frozen to death in the hours that you were in there but didn't even suffer frost burns to your ears. It meant you had to have lied or at least been mistaken about when you went in there. That's still not definitive, but I think you were only in there a short while. Long enough to get cold, but no longer.'

'There were other things too. You claimed to have trouble hearing the voices because of the leaves rustling on the breeze.' Albert raised his hands so people would look at the trees. It was full autumn and there wasn't a leaf in sight. 'You claimed your shoes were stolen by the robbers, but they weren't, were they? You got them muddy rushing back to the dairy and taking a short cut around the village. It was bad enough that you'd driven a truck through the village at night, but you weren't brave enough to risk walking back along the streets where someone getting a glass of water might look out of their window and see you. You went around the village; I spotted the little splashes of dirt on your trousers in the hospital. Really, though, it was when Oxford told you we'd tracked the criminal to a lockup in Fen Lane and invited you to join him. The life drained from your face when you ought to have been excited to get the cheese back. You thought you were caught already, and Rex here,' Albert patted the dog's head, 'he was trying to tell me where the cheese was. He could smell inside lockup number three and kept pawing at the door. Unfortunately, I don't always pay enough attention to what my dog is telling me. I still didn't know for certain, not until we came back through the village chasing someone else and I saw you heading to Fen Lane again. You were there last night, but the police were in Karl Tarkovsky's lockup. You couldn't risk trying to retrieve the truck, and you couldn't do it during the day, so you waited until dark again.'

'What was the coincidence?' asked Mr Brenner. Like everyone else, he'd listened with rapt fascination, but no one had picked up that tiny snippet of very important detail and he wanted to know the answer.

Oxford answered, 'Karl Somethingski.' A sea of quizzical faces stared back at him. 'Dave made a name up on the spot when I first interviewed him. It was a nothing name, he said he'd heard the robbers talking but hadn't seen any of their faces. Karl Somethingski, a nothing name intended to be unconnectable to anyone. Unfortunately for Dave, by blind coincidence, it led me to find a local criminal who owned a lockup full of stolen goods two up from the lockup containing the truck full of stolen Stilton. Karl was murdered just hours after the robbery took place.' The word murder caused a ripple of surprised murmuring. 'He was involved in a counterfeit ring run by my own chief inspector, a man most of you just saw me arrest. If Dave had said any other name, he most likely would have got away scot free and the chief inspector would have continued to make money unchecked.' He turned around and motioned for the crowd to part. 'Dave, I'm afraid I do not have any cuffs so I shall ask you to cooperate.' While the village listened, Oxford read Dave his rights and made his second arrest of the night and of his career.

Albert's stomach rumbled, which reminded him that Rex hadn't been fed. As they began back toward the dairy, someone sober driving the truck behind the possession of people, Albert said, 'You know what, lad. I think you'll make a darned good cop. If you moved to the city, you could go far.'

Oxford flipped his eyebrows. 'I think perhaps I'll just stay here. I think life in Stilton could be pretty great.'

The Aftermath

The villagers became a frenzied workforce that Friday night, throwing themselves into transforming the village into the festival-ready state it needed to be. A television crew from a local station was in the village, staying overnight to be up early for filming the next morning. They caught whiff of the activity somehow, arriving with their cameras, microphones, and an attractive man in a good suit to ask the questions.

Mr Brenner proved himself astute enough to recognise an opportunity, throwing his jacket off and rolling up his sleeves as he mucked in with cheesemaker, truck driver, and stallholder alike. They quickly made a point of filming him as he dug into a drain to dig out some litter. However, they failed to capture the bitter disappointment on his face when half a dozen police cars swept into the village to distract them. They abandoned filming the dairy boss getting his hands dirty in favour of a much bigger story. It wasn't missed by Tom though, who laughed raucously and cared not if it cost him his job.

Oxford's call for back up resulted in dozens of cops descending on the village. They came to get the chief inspector and look for a man called Albert Smith who had, according to three senior officers in Kent, just solved a double murder, and foiled a money-counterfeiting ring.

The TV crew followed the flashing lights to the cottage where someone had found a tea light to illuminate the blue police light above the door. It gave the cottage a romantic appearance from a distant point in time.

The senior officer on scene was a detective superintendent by the name of Singleton and he was astute enough to recognise the benefit to his career a little bit of TV time could do. Finding Albert and getting some of the back story from one of his subordinates, he said, 'Mr Smith, I'm going to start the press conference shortly, sir. I'll invite you to join me once I have made a preliminary statement.'

'What about PC Shaw?' Albert asked. 'Surely he is the one they should be interviewing.'

Detective Superintendent Singleton checked over his shoulder to make sure no one was listening. 'Listen, the lad's a bit of a joke at the station in Peterborough. His dad was ... well, let's just say he wasn't a very good police officer and his kid isn't doing very well for himself either.'

'But he just caught his own chief inspector. Shaw's father ruined his own career attempting to prove the man was bent and now the son has completed the job. I'd say that ought to exonerate the father, wouldn't you?'

Taken aback, Singleton nevertheless didn't agree. 'I don't think so. It's too late to undo what is now more than a decade old. Some things stick.'

Two minutes later, corralling the TV crew so he could control who they filmed, he asked Albert to come forward.

Albert really didn't want to, but he did it anyway because he recognised his obligation to set the record straight. The detective superintendent had no idea what was coming, and it disappointed Albert that a man who reached the same rank he had at the pinnacle of his career was so interested in media exposure.

With a microphone under his nose, the reporter in his fine suit asked, 'How did you manage to crack this case?'

Albert smiled as the reporter thrust the microphone his way and took a pace to his left to get some distance between him and Singleton. 'I didn't. I have been acting as observer and advisor only. The hero of this story is a young man called Oxford Shaw. My role in uncovering the identity of the killer, a bent cop who PC Shaw's father suspected many years ago, is minor. I think we should invite him to answer your questions.'

Singleton made a grab for the microphone; this wasn't the way he wanted the press conference to go at all.

'Rex, guard,' whispered Albert as he wrapped his hand tightly around the lead and held on.

The TV crew caught the whole thing as the detective superintendent was bowled over backward by the giant dog who was then called to heel again by the strangely serene and confident old man.

'Are you there, Oxford?' asked Albert. Oxford shook his head; he didn't want to go in front of the cameras. 'It's time to set the record straight, lad.'

Now caught in the spotlight as the cameras pinned him in place, Oxford said a prayer to his father and let it happen.

When the cameras swung away from him, Albert tucked himself away to one side with Rex, leaning against the wall of the house out of shot as he listened to Oxford take all the credit. In the two minutes when Singleton was making sure the TV crew had the perfect shot that he wanted, Albert had taken the lad to one side and told him exactly how it was going to go. Albert didn't want to be credited; he had no way of exchanging the credit for anything worthwhile. Not at his age. Oxford, however, could get his dad's name cleared, get the respect he deserved and just maybe get a medal to pin on the wall.

Singleton wanted back into the shot, but the TV crew had no interest in him. The West Indian kid had a great back story to go with the incredible tale of murderers, counterfeiters, and stolen cheese. Everyone, cops included, listened with rapt fascination to the convoluted tale. Albert knew the police public relations people would be going nuts at the negative exposure this was bringing – a senior officer embroiled in murder and counterfeiting while covering up his own crimes by leading the investigation. He didn't care though; he'd always been a fan of the truth.

In the quiet that followed the TV crew's departure, Oxford was able to hand off his two detainees – there was nowhere to keep them at the cottage – and settle down to several hours of paperwork. He would be on the ten o'clock news and probably on the front page of a local paper, there might be a commendation in the offing, but his focus for the weekend was to get the cottage looking spick and span before his new sergeant arrived on Monday.

Weary from his day, Albert walked Rex back to the pub where he rested on a bar stool and ate chicken and chips in a basket with a pint of Belgian lager and a half pint for Rex: he felt the dog deserved it.

Rex was thoroughly enjoying his time with his human. Every day seemed to be a new adventure and he wondered where they might get to next.

When they slept that night, they both snored loud enough to keep the couple in the next room awake.

The Festival

I n the morning, at breakfast, Albert could hear the couple at the next table discussing something that had happened in the village the previous evening.

'I don't know what was going on,' said the lady, 'but there were half a dozen police cars going through the village. I do hope the festival won't be affected; they've got such nice weather for it this year.'

Overhearing them as he brought their breakfasts out, his hands wrapped in tea towels to protect them from the hot plates, Gerald said, 'Don't you worry. Nothing could ever stop the Stilton festival from happening.'

Albert popped a piece of sausage in his mouth with a smile.

The festival was a roaring success, and though he kept trying to pay for things, all the stallholders insisted in giving Albert their wares for free. By late morning, he could feel his stomach pushing against his belt. He was in no rush, planning to stay to watch the cheese race at noon and then find a good place to sit to idly watch the world go by, but soon it would be time to push on. He was due in Bedford for supper where he expected to have a quiet time learning to bake the Bedfordshire Clanger, a savoury pudding not unlike, but never to be confused with, a Cornish pasty. His Stilton adventure was coming to a close, but he couldn't consider moving on without speaking with Oxford one last time.

He had to find a police officer to help him locate PC Shaw, but the young female officer recognised Albert from the television the previous evening and was only too happy to use her radio to bring Oxford to her location.

Albert waited with her, chatting amiably until he saw Oxford approaching. In contrast to his expectations, Oxford hadn't been given an unwanted task directing traffic at the edge of the village, he'd been asked to perform the most important role at the festival: firing the starter's gun to set the cheese racers in motion. That was happening in less than twenty minutes, so he had to be quick.

'You should come to the start line,' he suggested. Then to his female colleague said, 'Thanks for taking care of him, Megan.'

He got a wink in response and as the men, one old one young, made their way back up the High Street to the cheese race start point, Albert chose to rib the younger man. 'So that's Megan is it?'

Oxford couldn't stop the goofy grin from forming. 'Yeah. I kind of like her.'

Albert nodded in appreciation. 'I can see why.' He fell silent, but after a moment said, 'I'll be going soon, lad. I just wanted to say goodbye. It's been quite good fun visiting Stilton. I expected to eat some Stilton and maybe see how they make the cheese.'

'You never did get the factory tour, did you?'

Albert smiled. 'No, Oxford. I didn't. I got something better. I made a friend.'

Mrs Graves came bustling across the road, clutching her clipboard, and looking just as flustered as she had every other time Albert had seen her. 'Constable Shaw, it's almost time, we need to get you to the start point.'

Oxford laughed and rushed after her, waving to Albert that he shouldn't go anywhere, and they would be able to chat soon.

Albert positioned himself at the end of the road, twenty yards down from the start point where he had a great view. There were a dozen teams lined up, all with a cheese at their feet and beaming smiles on their faces.

Unable to wipe the smile from his face, he ruffled the fur on Rex's head and gave the dog a hug. 'Are you ready, boy? Are you ready?'

Rex looked up at his human. 'Ready? Ready for what?' his tail wagged. 'Are we about to play a game?'

The gun went off, Oxford starting the race on the stroke of noon and the over-excited teams exploded into action, wheeling their whole Stilton cheeses along the High Street to the joyous cheers of the watching crowd.

He was ready. He was ready!

As the first cheese came level, he lunged.

'Rex, no!'

Epilogue — The Gastro Thief

The exquisite porcelain cup of kopi luwak coffee hit the wall and exploded, showering the mink fur carpet with hot, brown liquid that cost four hundred dollars a pound.

On his television was the evening news which was showing a human-interest article about a dog wrecking the Stilton festival's traditional cheese rolling race. That wasn't what had his attention. His television was paused on the image of the man chasing after the dog. The name Albert Smith was already indelibly etched into his brain.

'You denied me my cheese, Albert Smith,' the man growled. 'How am I to survive the coming apocalypse without Stilton? I have Spillers & Bakers Pilot crackers that survived the Titanic to enjoy it with, but no Stilton.'

He looked around for something else to throw in anger but all he had within arm's reach was a throw cushion and the effect of it bouncing lightly off the wall would be unsatisfactory.

There were other delicacies to collect, of course. Many of them, and he already had more food in storage than he could possibly eat in his lifetime, but he appeared to be the only one who knew the end of the world was coming and he was going to live out the rest of his life without going hungry.

Hungry. Such an odd concept.

He spent half of his family's fortune building a bunker that would ensure his survival, and now he was stocking it with the foods that he wanted to savour while the rest of the human race perished on the surface. Among the list of foods he had to have was Stilton, and how was he to get it now?

He could try again, but they would be more wary now. He would have to arrange to have David Thornwell silenced before he could point anyone in his direction, but that was an entirely secondary matter when compared to his need to seek retribution on Albert Smith.

'I may not have my cheese, Albert, but I will have my revenge.'

The End

Author's Note

T his is another one of those books which grew from a simple idea into a monster with arms and legs. I don't plot much before I start writing; that's just the way I do it, and I have learned that I am fairly unusual in this. I let the stories tell themselves. I let the characters talk to me as I write, and they develop their own story arcs as they grow.

In my few pages of notes as I set out to craft this story, Dave was the sidekick for Albert throughout the story, but quite early on, I created Oxford and quite unexpectedly had a more versatile character who I felt a connection to. Dave was always going to be the cheese thief, a foolish man tempted by the lure of money he wasn't prepared to work for, but he took a back seat to Oxford, though I am sure he forgives me.

The chief inspector was going to be an annoying character who would be made to look small when Albert solved the case, but yet again, he chortled at me with a vaudevillian laugh and announced himself as the bad guy when I was about sixty percent of my way through the book. It made the story feel not only more complete but also more surprising and I love to finish with a big scene that chews up fifteen to twenty percent of the book as I enter the end narrative. I would struggle to explain the joy I have writing the end scenes of each book as everything comes together.

Do they have mushy peas outside of the UK? I honestly don't know but will confess that I love them. The first memory I have of this odd delicacy was at a pub in Wiltshire (literally the middle of nowhere) when the eighteen-year-old author in hiding, was a young soldier on a caving expedition to develop his adventurous side. Served a dish of faggots and mushy peas – faggots are like a meatball but a true peasant dish which hasn't been correctly made if one fails to find an artery poking out, or perhaps a tooth contained within. They are the inedible bits scraped from the floor of the butcher's shop and served on a bed of mushy peas at the end of a day when a person has expended several thousand calories, they are sublime.

It is a gorgeous summer day here in the southeast of England. My lawn is looking brown, but the rest of the garden is blooming as are my wonderful children and beautiful wife. Life is grand and I have more to be thankful for than one man deserves.

I will close this out now because I have a different set of characters demanding my attention. It's the Blue Moon bunch and I need to set free their next story. Undead Incorporated, much like this story, has a couple of pages of notes, which forms a skeleton for the story. How it turns out ... well, that's down to the characters as they help me commit to page what happens in their world.

Take care

Steve Higgs

History of the Dish

With its distinctive blue veins, Stilton has a long heritage as a cheese of quality, although its origins remain unknown. A large, drum-shaped cheese sits proudly on a table. With its crumble-cream texture, soft, butter-yellow crust, and distinctive blue veins, this is Stilton.

Today, Stilton enjoys Protected Designation of Origin (PDO) status. This dictates that it can only be produced in the counties of Nottinghamshire, Derbyshire and Leicestershire, to a legally binding recipe. Each batch must pass strict quality controls. If one fails, it can only be sold as unnamed 'blue cheese'. Just six dairies are licensed to create this sumptuous, tangy cheese, while a seventh makes only white Stilton. None of them are in, or even near, the village of Stilton in Cambridgeshire from which its name comes.

Accidental process

For many years, it was claimed that Stilton cheese did not originate in the eponymous village. Recent research, however, has fetched up a recipe dated 1722. This implies that a cheese called Stilton was made in the village in the early 18th century. As a white, pressed, cream cheese, it bore little resemblance to the product known today.

No one knows for certain, but it is believed the distinctive blue veining may have happened by accident. As it aged, the cheeses produced natural cracks into which mould spores would develop. Far from being repulsed, early connoisseurs were delighted by this. The cheese's flora and fauna are at their most active in and around the rind, ensuring flavour at its most complex. Daniel Defoe, writing in 1724, said he had "pass'd Stilton, a village famous for cheese, which is call'd our English Parmesan, and is brought to table with the mites, or maggots round it, so thick, that they bring a spoon with them for you to eat the mites with, as you do the cheese."

It is unknown what made the cheese mites so tasty to 18th century travellers. While Stilton today is made to methods that remain traditional, modern hygiene standards ensure the rind remains maggot-free.

Coaching trade

Stilton cheese's fame spread. This may have been because it was made with whole milk and extra cream, unlike many cheaper cheeses where part-skimmed milk was used. Geography also played a large role. Sitting on the Great North Road, Stilton was only seventy miles from London. This made it a convenient stopping point for coaches travelling north to York or further. At its height, Stilton was heaving with humanity and horses. A minimum of three hundred horses were held at The Bell Inn, with three hundred more at The Angel. These would be changed with the tired horses of coaches travelling through. There were a further fourteen hostelries in the village, all with accommodation.

Visitors would be aware of Stilton's large cheese market, held every Wednesday. In 1743, Cooper Thornhill, landlord of The Bell, had an idea. He began working with Frances Pawlett, a cheesemaker from Wymondham, Leicestershire, to make something truly special on a more commercial scale. It is claimed Pawlett came up with a novel way to avoid having to press the whey from her cheeses. She moulded them in ceramic pipes, fired with holes, from which the fluid could drain. It also gave the product the classic drum-shape it retains till this day. Pawlett set out high standards for her 'Stilton' cheese, giving it an early reputation for quality.

Christmas tradition

At first, Cooper Thornhill served it to guests, then sold it to passing travellers. Finally, as news of its superior quality spread, he began supplying Stilton to fashionable cheesemongers in London.

Traditionally, the cheese was made in the summer months, when the local pasture and, therefore, milk was at its richest. The rounds didn't mature until December, but this made them perfect for Christmas. Stilton's rich creaminess is still associated with the season's feast.

The arrival of steam railways killed the coaching trade and Stilton's hotel business. The cheese industry, though, flourished thanks to improved distribution. However, all six of today's Stilton dairies remain within a few miles of each other in the crook of three counties.

In the 1790s, the cheese sold at half a crown a pound, twice a day's wages for an average farm worker. Top quality ingredients and an intense hands-on process mean it continues to be the luxury product it has always been.

Making Stilton Cheese

Approximately 16 gallons (72 litres) of milk are needed to make a prime 16lb 8oz (7.5kg) whole cheese. Everything, from the breed of the cow to its health and what it eats, will affect both flavour and texture. To meet the requirements of the Protected Designation of Origin, cattle must be grazed within a certain area.

When Leicestershire cheesemaker Frances Pawlett created Stilton in the 18th century, her milk would have been raw, direct from the cow. Modern Stilton uses pasteurised milk. This is cooled in giant vats, before it is introduced to a live starter culture of friendly bacteria, along with penicillium roqueforti. These are the mould spores that will eventually develop the blue veins. Traditionally, Stilton's clotting agent has been animal rennet, but in recent years a vegetarian alternative has also been made.

The cheesemaker's skill

A fine Stilton takes between 10 and 12 weeks from the moment the milk is pasteurised. Most processes are still done by hand. These include mixing the milk in the vats and cutting the curds to ladling, milling or grinding the curds into soft crumbs, and salting. Giant hoops are filled by hand to create the characteristic, cylindrical Stilton shape. There are no machines that can accurately check curds for setting point, or the developing cheeses for quality. This means the skills of individual cheesemakers are tested on a daily basis.

The cheeses are stored in the 'hastening' room in hoops similar to the moulds Frances Pawlett developed more than two hundred years ago. Over four to six days the whey slowly drains away, ensuring the cheeses will not collapse when they are de-hooped. The next process is to smooth them. The master cheesemaker strokes each cheese round to create a smooth crust. This prevents oxygen activating the blue spores too early.

The rounds are stored in a maturing room to develop the creamy, leathery crust essential for all Stilton cheeses. Variables such as temperature and humidity decide exactly how long each batch will take.

For five weeks they are turned regularly to allow the air to reach each round evenly. Then they are individually pierced with steel needles to introduce air. This activates the mould spores for the blue veins. The blue does not develop in the pierced holes, but in tiny cracks and fissures within the cheese's loose, crumbly body. The cheese rounds see out their maturation in the blueing store, for between four and six weeks. Here again, they are regularly turned and graded with a long coring tool, or iron, to ensure quality.

Serving Stilton

Some strange misconceptions have grown up around how Stilton should be served. It is best cut simply, in wedge-shaped slices. The general advice is to 'cut high, cut low, cut level'. This involves cutting a small wedge in the top, about ½in (1cm) deep. Cutting is continued around it like a shallow cake, slicing it off horizontally to ensure the least amount of air reaches the main body. Scooping exposes more surface area to the air. This dries out the cheese, killing both flavour and texture. It is not recommended if the cheese is not to be eaten at one sitting. Nosing the cheese, that is removing the soft, creamy inner 'nose' leaving fellow diners with the hard crust, is not acceptable.

Stilton village's guide to eating this most tricky of cheeses claims the high cream content not only renders butter unnecessary, it detracts from the experience, making it over-rich.

Recipe : Stilton Cheese Scones

Ingredients:

225g/9 oz self-raising flour

50g/2 oz cold unsalted butter cut into small cubes

1 teaspoon baking powder

½ teaspoon English mustard powder

½ teaspoon salt150ml

/¼ pint milk plus extra for glazing

50g/2 oz Stilton cheese grated

Enough grated mature cheddar cheese for sprinkling on the top of each scone (approx' half an ounce or a quarter of a cup)

Makes 6 to 8 scones depending on the size of your cutter.

Method:

Preheat the oven 200c/190c fanGrease, with butter, a large baking sheet then dust with a little flour.

Sieve the flour, mustard powder and salt in a large bowl and mix together. Now, working quickly, add the cubed butter rubbing it into the flour using your fingertips until you have a mixture that resembles fine breadcrumbs, the reason you need to work quickly is because your fingers will start to warm the butter. Once the mixture resembles fine breadcrumbs using a dinner knife mix in the Stilton cheese cutting any large lumps of cheese up as Stilton is a soft cheese that doesn't grate well.

Now make a well in the centre and add nearly all the milk and stir it with the knife to get a soft pliable dough, add a little more milk if the dough is too dry, or a little more flour if it's too sticky – this does come with experience, but think of a very light playdough!

Turn the dough out onto a lightly floured surface and knead, very lightly, until it is smooth. Don't over work it, all you need to do is bring the dough together.

Next, rollout the dough to a thickness of 2cm/¾ inch and using a 7.5cm/3-inch cutter, dusted with some flour to stop it sticking, cut out the scones. Don't twist the cutter, as this will stop the scone from rising, but just lift the cutter out and place the scone on the prepared baking sheet.

Brush the tops, but not the sides, with milk and sprinkle on some grated cheddar cheese. Place in the oven for 15 minutes or until golden brown and cooked.

What's Next For Albert and Rex?

B aking. It can get a guy killed.

In the small Bedfordshire town of Biggleswade,
retired detective Albert, and former police dog, Rex, are enjoying a peaceful
break from the murder and mayhem of the last week. Until the waitress serving
him is arrested for murder ...

... and he discovers she killed the café's owner
three days ago.

But Albert saw her eyes when the police came for
her – she is innocent! With evidence stacked against her, no alibi, and both
motive and opportunity, she will carry the blame unless someone can prove
otherwise.

Left holding her dog when the police took her
away, Albert does what he does best ... he snoops. There is something
very odd
going on, that's for sure, but as he starts to investigate, the woman's
checkered past comes to life. Is she guilty after all?

In no time at all Albert becomes the target and
this time it will take more than Rex to keep him safe.

Is there a master criminal working behind the
scenes? What possible motive could he have? One thing is for sure ...
this is no
underdog tale!

Bedfordshire Clanger Calamity

ALBERT SMITH'S CULINARY CAPERS

STEVE HIGGS

Blue Moon Investigations

Paranormal Nonsense
The Phantom of Barker Mill
Amanda Harper Paranormal Detective
The Klowns of Kent
Dead Pirates of Cawsand
In the Doodoo With Voodoo
The Witches of East Malling
Crop Circles, Cows and Crazy Aliens
Whispers in the Rigging
Bloodlust Blonde – a short story
Paws of the Yeti
Under a Blue Moon – A Paranormal
Detective Origin Story
Night Work
Lord Hale's Monster
The Herne Bay Howlers
Undead Incorporated
The Ghoul of Christmas Past
The Sandman
Jailhouse Golem
Shadow in the Mine

Patricia Fisher Cruise Mysteries

The Missing Sapphire of Zangrabar
The Kidnapped Bride
The Director's Cut
The Couple in Cabin 2124
Doctor Death
Murder on the Dancefloor
Mission for the Maharaja
A Sleuth and her Dachshund in Athens
The Maltese Parrot
No Place Like Home

Felicity Philips Investigates

To Love and to Perish
Tying the Noose
Aisle Kill Him
A Dress to Die For

Patricia Fisher Mystery Adven

What Sam Knew
Solstice Goat
Recipe for Murder
A Banshee and a Bookshop
Diamonds, Dinner Jackets, and
Frozen Vengeance
Mug Shot
The Godmother
Murder is an Artform
Wonderful Weddings and Dea
Divorces
Dangerous Creatures

Patricia Fisher: Ship's Detective

The Ship's Detective
Fitness Can Kill

Albert Smith Culinary Cape

Pork Pie Pandemonium
Bakewell Tart Bludgeoning
Stilton Slaughter
Bedfordshire Clanger Calami
Death of a Yorkshire Puddin
Cumberland Sausage Shocke
Arbroath Smokie Slaying
Dundee Cake Dispatch
Lancashire Hotpot Peril
Blackpool Rock Bloodshed

Realm of False Gods

Untethered magic
Unleashed Magic
Early Shift
Damaged but Powerful
Demon Bound
Familiar Territory
The Armour of God
Live and Die by Magic
Terrible Secrets

Printed in the USA
CPSIA information can be obtained
at www.ICGtesting.com
LVHW011918240124
769894LV00007B/443